W9-CLS-202

Also by Nancy Bell
in Large Print:

ggie and the Poisoned Politician

Biggie
and the
Meddleso
Mailma

Biggie
and the
Meddlesome
Mailman

Nancy Bell

Thorndike Press • Thorndike, Maine

Published in 2000 by arrangement with St. Martin's Press.

Thorndike Press Large Print Mystery Series.

The tree indicium is a trademark of Thorndike Press.

The text of this Large Print edition is unabridged.
Other aspects of the book may vary from the original edition.

Set in 16 pt. Plantin by Susan Guthrie.

Printed in the United States on permanent paper.

Library of Congress Cataloging-in-Publication Data

Bell, Nancy, 1932–
    Biggie and the meddlesome mailman / Nancy Bell.
        p. cm.
    ISBN 0-7862-2552-l (lg. print : hc : alk. paper)
        1. Biggie (Fictitious character : Bell) — Fiction.
2. Women detectives — Texas — Fiction. 3. Grandmothers —
Fiction. 4. Texas — Fiction. 5. Large type books. I. Title.
PS3552.E5219 B545 2000
813′.54—dc21   00-028644

To the Shoal Creek Writers,
Karen Fitzgerall, Dena Garcia, Eileen Joyce,
Sharon Kahn, and Judy Austin Mills

Willie Mae's Independence Day Coconut Pie

3 cups milk from fresh coconut and sweet milk
1 cup sugar
½ cup cornstarch
¼ teaspoon salt
3 egg yolks, beaten
2 cups grated fresh coconut
½ teaspoon almond extract
1 teaspoon vanilla extract
1 baked pie shell
1 cup whipping cream with a little sugar

Measure the milk you get from the coconut and add in enough sweet milk to make up three cups. Dump it all in a pot and start it heating on the stove. While that's getting hot (watch it; you don't want it to boil!) mix together your sugar, cornstarch, and salt. Gradually add that into your milk in the pot. Keep stirring until it's all smooth and mixed together good. Boil that for about two minutes, stirring. Take the pot off the heat and set it aside while you beat up your egg yolks; then stir a little of the hot stuff into your eggs. Be careful or you'll end up with scrambled eggs. Now add your egg mixture back into the pot and cook, stirring, over a low fire until it gets thick enough to coat your spoon. Generally, that takes about five minutes. Turn it out into a bowl and add in half your coconut and your extracts. Now pour it into your cooked piecrust. Cover with plastic wrap — push it down over the custard so it won't form a skin — and put it in the icebox for a good long time until it gets cool. To serve, whip cream with a little sugar to taste and spread it over the pie. Sprinkle on the rest of your coconut and stand back. Your family will run right over you to get to that pie.

NOTE: Willie Mae says if you don't take along an ice chest, don't take this pie to a picnic. It needs to be kept cool or somebody might get sick.

Job's Jottings from Julia

June 12. Good news for the James Royce Wooten Chapter of the Daughters of the Republic of Texas. Biggie Weatherford, president, tells this reporter that the Lions Club has donated a nice piece of land out near the lake to our chapter. Seems they bought it for deer hunting, but their wives all got together and vetoed the idea. Ella Mae Riddle reports that the women objected to the project on the grounds that the Lions, all on the dark side of seventy, don't have a lick of business sitting outside in some drafty old deer blind in all kinds of weather, catching their death of cold, or worse. The Daughters plan to convert the property into a retreat center as soon as funds can be raised.

H.C. Crouch, formerly of Mount Vernon, has moved to town and started up a brand-new newspaper that will run my column from now on. H.C. brings to the job extensive experience in the newspaper business. He sold ads for the *Greenville Green Sheet* for four years before taking the position of assistant editor for the *Franklin County Weekly*

Shopper. You can pick up your copy of the *Kemp County Times* at the Owl Café, Plumley's Rexall, the Eazee Freeze, or the Fresh as a Daisy Café out on the bypass. H.C. will be calling on all you businesspeople up and down the square to sell you some advertising space. H.C. says his motto is: "Take an Ad in the *Times* and Rake in the Dimes."

My mister and I rode out to Buddy's Bait Shop for a barbecue plate last Saturday night. If you haven't been for a while, you ought to go. Buddy has got his son-in-law, Arvel, doing the cooking and, I'm telling you, those ribs just fall apart in your hands — and his pinto beans cooked up with little bits of jalapeño peppers will make you slap your grandpa.

Congrats to our mailman, Luther Abernathy. He's just received his ten-year pin for service to the PO. Luther tells me he's never missed a day's work since he signed on with the postal service way back when.

Well, that's all for now. Remember, if you have any tidbits for this column, you can find me at the newspaper office next door to the barbershop on the square.

1

It was early June and the crepe myrtle was dropping pink flowers all over the place when Prissy Moody bit a chunk out of our mailman, Luther Abernathy. School had been out almost a week. I was waiting on the front steps for Luther to bring some sea monkeys I'd ordered out of the back of a magazine. I planned on raising sea monkeys and selling them to the other kids when school started in the fall. I figured by that time I'd have a pretty fair-sized herd and could sell them for, probably, a dollar fifty a head. I watched as Luther, who is slow as molasses in January, made his way down the street toward our house. He must have spent a whole hour standing on the porch jawing with Mrs. Muckleroy, who lives at the end of our block. Everybody says Luther could talk the hide off a cow.

Our house sits right square in the middle of the block on Elm Street in Job's Crossing, Texas. It's called Elm Street on account of elm trees line both sides of the street and meet in the middle. That's not to say we don't have plenty of dogwoods and redbuds and magnolias, too. All the houses were built a long time ago and are white, with front porches and big yards. The yards all have terraces in front, so you have to go up three or four steps before you even get to the front sidewalks that lead up to the houses. Those are the steps I was sitting on while I waited for Luther.

After stopping to chat with everybody and their brother up and down our block, Luther finally made it to Mrs. Moody's next-door. I figured it wouldn't be long now, because I'd seen Mrs. Moody get in her car and drive off not ten minutes ago. He'd have to come on over to our house on account of he wouldn't have anybody to talk to there. The trouble was, when he opened the iron gate in front of Mrs. Moody's house, Prissy Moody ran out from under a cape jasmine bush and chomped down hard on his ankle.

Luther, who is six-foot-four and shaped like a question mark, let out a yell and commenced dancing around and shaking his foot. Prissy, who won't weigh four pounds soaking wet, must have been feeling tough that day, because she just growled and hung on tighter. Finally, Luther gave up trying to shake her loose and, after dropping Mrs. Moody's mail in her box, started toward our house with Prissy still hanging on.

"Don't that hurt?" I asked as he came wobbling up our walk dragging Prissy behind him.

"Not anymore," Luther said. "See, she's done let go of my meat. Now, she's just got ahold of my pants leg."

I looked down at Prissy, who rolled her eyes at me and started shaking her head as fast as she could, like she was trying to tear off a piece of Luther's gray postman's pants. Luther commenced digging in his leather bag for our mail.

"I see you got your sea monkeys," he said, handing me a little brown envelope.

I took the envelope and frowned at Luther. "How come you know this is sea monkeys?" I asked. "Anyway, this can't be them. In the picture, they were big and had little smiley faces."

"Oh, that's them all right," Luther said. "What you gotta do, you gotta put them in water; then they'll swell up and come alive."

I started to tear open the envelope and noticed it had already been opened and stuck back together with tape.

"Be careful," Luther said. "You don't want them sea monkeys to fall out."

Just then my grandmother, Biggie, who is called Biggie on account of I couldn't say

13

"Big Momma" when I was a little kid, came to the front door. "Afternoon, Luther," she said. "Got anything for me? I'm expecting a very important letter from a state senator in Austin."

Luther shook his head. "Nothin' from a senator," he said. "Here's a letter from the Daughters' headquarters, though. Looks important. And here's your light bill. Y'all need to cut down, Miss Biggie. Mrs. Moody's bill ain't half what y'all's is. I just gave J.R. his sea monkeys, and that's it." He handed Biggie her mail. "Mrs. Muckleroy got a very important letter, though," he said. "It seems her godmother, a high-up society lady from Nacogdoches, passed on and left all her wigs to Mrs. Muckleroy. You see, the old lady had lost most of her hair and had as fine a collection of wigs as you'll find west of the Sabine River."

Biggie covered her mouth to hide a smile. "You don't say," she said.

Luther pushed his hat back and scratched his head. "I'm so dry, I'm spittin' cotton," he said. "You don't reckon Willie Mae would spare me a drop of iced tea, do you?"

"Of course," Biggie said, "and while you're drinking it, I'll just take a look at that ankle of yours." She disappeared into the house and came right back carrying a fishbowl

14

glass full of tea with a sprig of mint sticking out the top. She was also carrying a box of bandages and a bottle of rubbing alcohol. "I put in six spoons of sugar, just like you like it," she said, handing him the tea. "Now, let's have a look at your leg."

I almost felt sorry for Luther. When Biggie decides to doctor you, she goes whole hog. I remember once when I fell off my bike and skint myself up real bad, she painted a whole lot of iodine on me. It wouldn't wash off. My teacher kept sending home notes saying she thought Biggie should have my liver checked on account of I was so yellow.

Luther sank down on the steps, holding the leg with Prissy attached out in front of him.

"My stars, honey," Biggie said, "I can't do a thing with that dog hanging onto you."

"She won't turn loose," I said. "She thinks she's caught a big old snake."

"Hmmm," Biggie said. "Why don't you just run in the house and fetch Booger. I saw him asleep on the dining table."

"Yeah!" I said, heading for the door.

Booger is my cat. He can beat Prissy up any time he takes the notion. Sure enough, when I brought Booger out he hopped up on the porch rail and stared down at Prissy like a buzzard on a limb. Prissy let go of Luther and commenced barking at Booger. Old Booger jumped down off the rail and started low-walking toward Prissy with his tail down. Prissy took off for her yard like her tail was on fire and hunkered down next to her front door shaking. Booger jumped back on the porch rail and commenced licking his left hind leg.

"Now, let's have a look at that ankle," Biggie said, squatting beside Luther. She raised his pants cuff up. "My gracious," she said, "it's already starting to swell. I'll just pour a little alcohol on it and —"

"No'm, that's all right. It ain't hurt bad. I'll take care of it when I finish my — ow! That hurts!"

Biggie had poured half a bottle of alcohol over his ankle.

"Now," she said, "I dare any germs to get to that. Hold still, honey, while I put a bandage on there."

"Thanks, I reckon," Luther said. He rubbed his ankle once, then continued talking just like he'd never been interrupted. "Truth is, I think Ruby Muckleroy was just a little disappointed, doncha know. It's my understanding that she thought she'd at least get the old lady's silver punch bowl."

"Do tell," Biggie said.

"Yes'm. That went to a niece that lived over in Lufkin. They tell the old lady hadn't even set eyes on her in thirty years."

"Um-hum," Biggie said.

"They was right nice wigs, though," Luther continued. "Come with stands and everything. . . ."

"More tea?" Biggie asked.

Luther stood up. "No'm," he said. "A postman's got his duties. I swan, all this junk mail's gonna make me old before my time. Would you believe Miss Oprah Lee got four of them Victoria's Secret catalogs in one week? And ever' one of um had a different gal on the cover dressed in nothin' but her underwear! I don't know — I just don't know. Well, I reckon I'd best be goin'."

Biggie took his hand and helped him up.

Luther started down the walk, then turned back. "By the way," he said, "are you takin' your car to Les's Auto Repair?"

"Why would I do that?" Biggie asked.

"When it's broke, I mean."

"Oh," Biggie said.

"It don't matter," Luther said. "I was just thinkin', you might want to give that poor feller some business now and then. Seem like every single day some creditor is sending him bills — second and third notices, too. Lately, I been noticin' letters from

17

collection agencies mixed up in old Les's mail."

"I'll give that some thought," Biggie said. "You take care now, Luther."

Luther headed down the sidewalk limping a little, his leather mailbag slippity-slapping against his back. Biggie shook her head as she watched him go. "I declare," she said, "when Luther dies, they'll have to take a stick and beat his tongue to death."

"That don't make sense, Biggie," I said. "If he's dead, ain't his tongue dead, too?"

"*Isn't*," Biggie said, "not *ain't*. And of course his tongue would be dead. It's just an expression. My goodness, you're literal-minded — just like your daddy."

My daddy was Biggie's son. He died when I was six. After the funeral Biggie brought me home to live with her on account of my mama being the high-strung type that couldn't take care of an active child like me. Mama lives in Dallas and is a cocktail waitress at the Autotel Ballroom on Harry Hines Boulevard.

I don't remember much about life with Mama and Daddy except that Daddy liked to joke and drink beer and Mama had to lie down a lot on account of her head was splitting. I asked her once if she wasn't worried her brains would leak out if her head split, but she just gave me a funny look and pulled a pillow over her face. Anyway I'm twelve now, and there's no place I'd rather be than right here in Job's Crossing with Biggie and Willie Mae and Rosebud.

Biggie is no bigger than a minute. She might not want me to tell you this, but she just had her sixtieth birthday last November. For an old lady she is very energetic. Just try to follow her around for one day, and you'll see what I mean. She can outwork any man twice her size. She has short, curly red hair, which she keeps that way by going to Itha's House of Hair every Wednesday afternoon at 3:00. I should mention that Biggie is a Very Important Person in town. That's on account of her ancestor, James Royce Wooten, who I'm named after. He was the first person to settle this town, and there is a statue of him in front of the courthouse. Biggie is president of the James Royce Wooten Chapter of the Daughters of the Republic of Texas.

The way we got Willie Mae was, she showed up at our back door one day. That was the day Codella, our last maid, had gone running off down the street hollering that the devil lived in our toilet. That was silly on account of it wasn't the devil at all in our

19

toilet. It was just an old catfish Biggie had put there for safekeeping until she had time to clean him. Biggie was about at the end of her rope because she couldn't find a maid that was willing to stay for more than a few days at our house. That's because Biggie has her own way of doing things. A lot of people don't understand that, but I do. I mean, like Biggie says, if you've got a whole bushel basket full of turnip greens, why wash them in the sink when the bathtub's bigger? And on a hot summer day, what's wrong with sitting with your feet propped in the refrigerator? Of course, she doesn't have to do that anymore, because last summer we put in air-conditioning.

Willie Mae walked into our house wearing a red turban and gold earrings. She had all her worldly possessions in a black satin pillowcase. She took one look at our kitchen and said, "Looks like I got here just in time." She pulled a starched white apron out of her pillowcase and started right in cleaning up the mess me and Biggie had made. You see, Biggie never had much time for housework what with her civic duties and fishing and all, and I was just a little kid and couldn't be expected to keep house.

By suppertime, Willie Mae had the house all spick-and-span and a big pot of gumbo gurgling on the stove. That night, Biggie and Willie Mae sat at the kitchen table drinking black Cajun coffee and talking until past midnight. The next day, Biggie and Willie Mae cleaned up the little guesthouse in the backyard and Willie Mae unpacked her pillowcase and moved right in. You wouldn't believe the stuff she pulled out of that pillowcase. Willie Mae is a voodoo woman, you see. She can do magic. I know. I've seen it.

Willie Mae hadn't been with us more than a month when her husband, Rosebud, got out of jail in Mansfield, Louisiana, and came to live with us. Rosebud is my best friend and also my Little League coach. He has gold hearts, clubs, diamonds, and spades built right into his four front teeth. Biggie put Rosebud to work taking care of the yard and driving her around.

That night after supper, Biggie said, "There's a nice breeze tonight. I believe I'll have my coffee on the front porch."

Pretty soon, we'd all followed her out. Willie Mae and Biggie sat on wicker rockers while Rosebud stretched out on the settee. I climbed up on the swing, which has blue-and-white striped cushions and is my favorite spot on the porch. For a while, we didn't say anything, just sat listening to the sound of the swing squeaking and Mrs. Moody's radio next-door as she listened to *Brother Dave's Holiness Gospel Hour Broadcast Live out of Del Rio, Texas.* The leaves made patterns on the pavement under the street lamp, and I watched as bats fluttered around the light catching bugs.

Finally, I said, "My sea monkeys came today."

"No foolin'," Rosebud said. "Where they at?"

"I got gypped," I said. "They're nothin' but some old dried-up pieces of nothin'. You think we could sue those people, Biggie?"

"How much money did you send them?" she asked.

"Nine ninety-eight plus three dollars shipping and handling," I said. "That's a lot of money, Biggie."

"Lemme see um," Rosebud said.

I dug the brown envelope out of my pocket and emptied the sea monkeys into Rosebud's palm.

Rosebud squinted at them, then brushed his palms together and watched while the wind blew my sea monkeys to kingdom come.

"What'd you do that for?" I asked.

"On account of you're right," he said. "You done got skint. Puts me in mind of the time my baby sister Rhonice sent off for one of them bust enhancers."

Willie Mae gave Rosebud a look, but he pretended not to see.

"A what?" I said.

"A bust enhancer, doncha know. Rhonice wasn't but thirteen, so she didn't have much out front, but she just ached to have a curvy figure like her best friend, Denise Dubois, who was a Creole girl and had more curves than a plate of spaghetti."

Rosebud sat up and pulled one of his smelly old cigars out of his shirt pocket. He lit it with a kitchen match and blew a dozen perfect smoke rings. Willie Mae made a face.

"Did it work?" I asked. "Did Rhonice get, uh . . ."

"I'm coming to that, ain't I?" Rosebud said. "Well, Rhonice sat on the front steps for six long weeks waiting for the mailman to come. When her package finally came, Rhonice had to pay sixty-seven cents postage due. Ooo-wee, that gal was so excited she couldn't hardly get the wrappin' off."

"What was it?" I asked. "Was it a gyp like my sea monkeys?"

"Well, no, I wouldn't go so far as to say

23

Rhonice got took on the deal. What it was, was a thing with handles on both ends that was joined together by a right stout spring. Rhonice had to stand in front of the mirror for thirty minutes every single night and push them handles together. The instructions had a picture of a gal with great old big ones. That's what kept Rhonice going — the thought that she could look just like that."

Willie Mae got up and stomped into the house, slamming the screen door behind her.

Rosebud grinned and continued. "Well, Rhonice, she stood in front of that mirror every single night pushin' and sweatin', but nothin' seemed to be happening. She was still just as flat as a mashed possum. I'll say this for my baby sister. She never did give up."

"Rosebud, you said she didn't get gypped. Sounds to me like she did. That thing was no good."

"That's where you're wrong, boy," Rosebud said. "You see, by the time Rhonice was seventeen, she still didn't have nothin' in front, but boy, her arms were as big as briskets. 'Long about that time, the wrasslin' matches come to town, and Rhonice and me went to see um." Rosebud laughed and slapped his knees. "It was their last night in town." He sniggered. "Amateur

24

Night, they called it. Wellsir, when they asked if anyone would like to get in the ring and wrassle the Thibedeaux Terminator, old Rhonice was on her feet raising one of her beefy old arms."

"Wow!" I said.

"That's right," Rosebud said, "and it didn't take but two rounds before Rhonice had terminated the Terminator. That's when Rhonice made up her mind. She was goin' to take up wrasslin' as a career. She joined the troupe and traveled all over the U.S. of A. and Canada billin' herself as the Bayou Bruiser. She beat every man in the business before it was revealed she was a woman. Well, naturally, after that the men wouldn't wrassle with her anymore."

"Why?" I asked.

"Why? Think, boy! Because it ud be too hoomilatin' to get counted out night after night by a woman," Rosebud said.

"Poor Rhonice," said Biggie, who had been listening to the story while she was pretending to read a magazine.

"Naw," Rosebud said. "Rhonice didn't care a bit. She'd already earned enough money to retire on and, like she said, too much wrasslin's hard on a woman's looks. She bought a nice little home in Mansfield and lives there to this day with her husband

25

and seven little flat-chested daughters."

"That's just great," I said, "but I don't see what it's got to do with me. I don't see much of a way for me to make a career out of those sea monkeys. Anyway, you threw them away."

"Then you wasn't listening," Rosebud said. "What Rhonice done was she took a bad thing and made something good out of it. You could do that, only you don't need them sea monkeys. You've already got something goin' for you, and you didn't have to send off for it."

"What?"

"Baseball, son. That's what. You could be the best right fielder on our team if you'd just quit goin' after pie in the sky and concentrate on the talent God's done give you." Rosebud stood up. "Now, go in the house and get your ball and glove. I feel like chunking a few before the moon comes up."

2

The next morning when I came down for breakfast, Rosebud was outside working in the front yard.

"Hurry up and eat," Willie Mae said, dumping a steaming apple cinnamon waffle on my plate. "You want bacon or sausage?"

"Is it the bacon Mr. Sontag made after he murdered Harvey?" I asked. Harvey was my friend Monica Sontag's pet pig.

"Yep," Willie Mae said. "What'll it be? I ain't got all morning."

"That's right," Biggie said, coming into the room and taking a seat at the table opposite me. "The Daughters are coming here tomorrow for a luncheon meeting. Willie Mae and I have a million things to do, and we're going to need all the help we can get." She reached for the maple syrup and poured half the pitcherful on the waffle Willie Mae set in front of her. "Umm-umm, Willie Mae, that looks good enough to make a bulldog break his chain."

"Is the sausage from the store?" I asked.

Willie Mae held up the package for me to see.

"I'll take four links," I said.

Willie Mae dumped the sausage on my plate and rumpled my hair with her other hand. "Put your napkin in your lap," she said.

I poked the sausage with my fork and thought about Harvey. Then I poured maple syrup on my waffle and gobbled it down in six bites. While Willie Mae and Biggie were talking about tomorrow's luncheon, I sneaked the sausages in my pocket. "I'll be right back," I said.

"Don't you go off," Biggie said. "I want you to help Rosebud clean out the flower beds and hose down the front of the house."

I went out the back door. Willie Mae's little house sits at the back of our yard and is connected to the back steps by a stone path with flower beds on both sides. Willie Mae keeps them planted with whatever flowers are in season. Now they were lined with yellow irises. A big mulberry tree stands next to the cottage with ivy hanging all over it. Rosebud says that ivy's gonna kill that tree, but Biggie says she'd rather have the ivy than the mulberry, which doesn't do anything but attract a bunch of blackbirds who eat the mulberries and then drop mulberry poop all over her car. She says she hopes the tree does die. There's a storm cellar on the other side of the yard, which is a place you can go to when a tornado is coming, but we never use it. I used to have a clubhouse in there, but it didn't work too well on account of every time it rains water gets caught in there. Biggie says she guesses that cellar will still be here long after the house is gone because it's made out of two feet of concrete. Our yard is separated from Mrs. Moody's by a white picket fence. I crossed over to the fence and, whistling softly, waited for Prissy to come. Sure enough, she crawled out from under her back steps and came tippy-toeing across the dewy grass, wagging her tail and yapping her shrill little bark. I took the sausages out of my pocket and stuck them between the pickets in the fence, just close enough so Prissy could smell them, but too far away for her to get her teeth into them. I had just settled down to watch Prissy digging under the fence and rooting after those sausages when Mrs. Moody came out her back door carrying a measuring cup. Mrs. Moody doesn't always bother to get dressed when she comes to our back door. This morning, she was wearing her raincoat over her nightgown and had on her son Wilson's Indian moccasin slippers that he got when he was in the army stationed in El Paso. Her hair was put up in pink rollers. She pushed open the gate between our yards and stepped over Willie Mae's jonquils.

"Bad dog," Mrs. Moody said to Prissy. "You're going to get all messy, and Mama will have to give you another bath." She pushed open the gate between the two yards. "Why, J.R.," she said. "I didn't see you there. Is Willie Mae in the kitchen? I'm just going over to see if I can borrow a cup of brown sugar."

I nodded and waited while she yoo-hooed her way through our back door and disappeared inside. Then I poked the sausages over to Prissy's side and followed Mrs. Moody into the kitchen.

"I know I look a sight," Mrs. Moody said. "But I had my mouth all fixed for pecan pie and decided I'd just get it in the oven before I had my bath. Well, wouldn't you just know it, I discovered I didn't have a speck of brown sugar left in the house." She sat down in a chair and took a swig of the Cajun coffee Biggie had poured for her and made a face. "Did y'all hear about Buddy Duncan?" she asked, pouring cream into her mug.

"What about him?" I asked. Buddy Duncan is a high school kid that owns his own motorcycle. One day he saw me admiring it in the parking lot at the Eazee Freeze and gave me a ride. I made up my mind that day that when I get to be a big kid in high school I'm going to be just like Buddy and always be nice to little kids.

"You mean Les Duncan's boy?" Biggie asked.

Mrs. Moody was shoveling sugar into her coffee. "The very same," she said. "His mama and daddy are mor'n likely fit to be tied. I know if it was my boy, Wilson . . . well, of course Wilson's grown and married now, but if Wilson had pulled a stunt like that when he was under my roof . . . I just know I wouldn't have been able to hold my head up in this town."

"Spit it out, Essie," Biggie said. "What did the boy do?"

"Well," Mrs. Moody said, "Luther told me all about it, and who else would know better what's going on in this town? I declare I'd just be as ignorant as an old billy goat if it wasn't for Luther. I guess we all would, wouldn't we, Biggie?"

"I expect so," Biggie said. "What did Luther say about Buddy?"

Mrs. Moody blew on her coffee and took a tiny sip. "It seems the boy got a letter from a judge over in Gregg County telling him his court case would be coming up on the first of

31

next month!" Mrs. Moody took another swig of coffee and leaned back to watch Biggie's reaction. When Biggie didn't say anything, she continued. "Luther said he imagined they'd throw the book at him on account of he's already got a criminal record from that time Delbert Clinton caught him and some other boys stealing sugarcane when they was in the seventh grade. You remember that? Anyway, the boy's in big trouble this time, for sure. The way I see it, some have just got the bad seed. Remember that movie, Biggie? That was the sweetest-looking little girl and so neat. But mean? That kid was meaner than a rattlesnake with a backache. Well, Luther says Buddy's probably the same way — all nicey-nicey on the outside and rotten to the core on the inside."

Biggie let out a long sigh. "Willie Mae," she said holding up her mug, "you'd better pour me another cup of coffee. It looks like Essie's got her tongue in high gear this morning."

Mrs. Moody grinned. "That puts me in mind of what Wilson's daddy used to say, God rest his sweet soul. He used to say, 'Esther, you must have been vaccinated with a Victrola needle.' He was a card, Wilson's daddy was. Anyway, you remember when there was a rash of hubcap robberies over in

32

Longview? It was in Julia Lockhart's column a month or so ago. It's been going on for upward of six months, I'd say. The whole town's been affected. Maybe you'd be parked at the mall, or church, or just in front of a friend's house, and you'd come out and — whoops! — there would be your hubcaps, just vanished into thin air. They tell it even happened to the sheriff's car parked right out in front of the courthouse. Well, as you may know, my sister Hester lives in Longview, and let me tell you the folks in that town are up to here with it. Hester lost hers in front of the post office when she wasn't in there more than five minutes! And believe you me, it's not easy to find replacements for a '56 Olds 98!" Mrs. Moody got up and helped herself to a glass out of the cabinet, opened the refrigerator, and poured herself some cold water. She sat back down at the table and went on talking. "Hubcaps were just flying off of cars all over town, and the police don't have a clue who's taking them."

"I heard something about that," Biggie said.

"Well," Mrs. Moody said, "Luther said Buddy and some of his friends went over to Longview one night last month. *Said* they were going to the picture show. *Said* they

33

didn't steal anything, just came out of the show and the police jumped them. Luther said everybody that believes that come see him on account of he's got some swampland down in Florida he'd like to talk to them about. That Luther's a card." She laughed and looked around to make sure everybody had got the joke, then continued talking. "Well, the whole thing pretty near put poor Mrs. Duncan in the hospital. Her heart's bad anyway. I know because they go to my church. Les, he's a deacon, and believe you me, it was all he could do to look folks in the eye when he passed the plate last Sunday. They have *got* to look folks in the eye you know, or a lot of them will try to pass off one folded-up dollar for a decent offering. Brother Puckett says an usher's got to keep on his toes or a church could go under in no time flat. He's seen it happen. He preached a real good sermon on that last year at Stewardship Sunday. Now, personally, I think it's a crying shame what that boy's gone and done to his poor mama and daddy."

"Hmmm," Biggie said. "That Luther's going to get in trouble one of these days, telling eveybody's business all over town. J.R., climb up on the counter and get down my cut-glass platter from the top shelf so Willie Mae can wash it for the luncheon tomorrow."

Mrs. Moody picked up her cup of brown sugar and headed out the back door looking real disappointed about the way her story had gone over.

"Bye, Essie!" Biggie called. "Now be careful, J.R.; I don't want you to fall. And take off your shoes first!"

I had to stand on tiptoe to reach the platter. It was propped up against the back wall behind two rows of mayonnaise jars and a big pile of margarine tubs Willie Mae was saving just in case we ever needed them. I was holding onto the shelf to steady myself. I got my hand on the platter and was bringing it out over the other stuff when something snapped and suddenly the little finger on my left hand felt like a snake had bitten it. I let out a holler and dropped the platter. I heard it smash on the floor just before I lost my balance and went tumbling after it.

Biggie just stood looking down at the mess on the floor. "It was my grandmother's," Biggie said. "It was a family heirloom."

"Ooowww!" I yelled. I held out my hand, and there, attached to my little finger, was a mousetrap.

"What?" Biggie looked at me like she'd forgotten I was there. "Oh, my soul," she said. She knelt down and carefully pulled the trap apart. I looked at my hand. The finger was already turning black.

"Let me see," Willie Mae said. She took some ice out of the refrigerator and wrapped it in a clean dish towel and gave it to me to hold around my finger, then ordered me to sit at the table until she and Biggie could get the glass cleaned up.

"Miss Biggie," Willie Mae said after my hand was bandaged and the mess was gone, "I seen a platter just like that in the window of that Dossie Phelps's antique store."

"You don't say," Biggie said. "I didn't know she had anything worth much in there. Of course, the windows are always so dusty, you can't see what's inside unless you go in, and I haven't had any reason to do that in a long time."

"Oh, no, Biggie," I said. "She's got good stuff. She's got an old Victrola that you have to wind up and a genuine belt buckle that belonged to Elvis and a camp stool that John Wesley Hardin, the famous outlaw, sat on —"

"In that case, maybe we can find ourselves a brand-new family heirloom. J.R., go out front and help Rosebud while I get dressed to go downtown."

I went upstairs to get my ball and glove and took them to the front porch. I sat on the steps watching while Rosebud raked up the ground around Biggie's big pecan tree. He was dressed the way he always is, in black dress pants and a white shirt. Dust from the leaves had covered his black shoes and the cuffs of his pants. "You're gonna get in trouble," I said.

Rosebud looked at me, leaning on his rake. "How come?" he asked.

"Look at your feet. You're getting all dirty. Rosebud, how come you don't wear work clothes to do yard work like everybody else?"

"Because I ain't everybody else," Rosebud said. "Go round to the shed and get the other rake. I need you to rake out them flower beds up next to the house."

After I'd raked up a big pile of sticks and rocks and cigar butts and gum wrappers, I went around back to find a basket to put them in. I couldn't find anything but Willie Mae's blue plastic clothes basket, so I took that off the back porch. Just as I was about to drop a big load of raked-up stuff into the basket, two things happened. Rosebud yelled, "Stop!" and DeWayne Boggs came walking pigeon-toed down the sidewalk toward our house.

"You want to get killed?" Rosebud asked. "Willie Mae'll have your head if you mess with her clean-clothes basket. Here, take one of these bags. Mornin', DeWayne."

DeWayne is short and pudgy and has skin the color of bread dough. His hair is the color of iron rust, and he wears it cut in a dorky burr. He lives in a little house on Compress Street with his mama, Betty Jo, and his brother, Franklin Joe, and his sister, Angie Jo. Betty Jo runs Itha's House of Hair, the beauty shop where Biggie gets her hair done. A lot of kids won't play with DeWayne, but I do sometimes on account of I feel sorry for him. He's had more hard luck than a kid ought to have.

"Hidy," DeWayne said. "Y'all want to throw some balls?"

"Wouldn't hurt," Rosebud said, dropping his rake where he stood. "Come on over in the side yard. Toss me the ball, J.R."

Me and DeWayne took our places at the far end of the side yard. Rosebud, at the other end, wound up to throw out the first ball. Just then, the dining room window came up and Willie Mae's head appeared.

"GET BACK TO WORK!"

Willie Mae motioned for me to come back in the house. I picked up the ball and headed for the front door. DeWayne followed me inside.

"Ain't we gonna practice? We ought to be practicin', J.R."

"Shut up," I said.

DeWayne followed me into the dining room, where Willie Mae stood with her hands on her hips. The dining table was covered with newspapers. On top of that were Biggie's silver tea service silver bowls and trays. Beside the silver sat a big jar of Wright's Silver Polish and a bunch of clean white rags.

"When you get through," Willie Mae said, "put all the silver on the buffet and throw the rags in my clothes basket. I'll go get it."

I was already halfway out the front door. "Never mind!" I called. "I know where it is."

Willie Mae shook her head and went back to the kitchen. I tossed DeWayne a rag and showed him how to polish.

DeWayne shook his head and headed for the door. "I gotta go," he said.

"It's fun," I said. "Watch here how it makes the rag turn black. Boy, I just love to polish silver."

"You do?" He came closer to the table.

"Sure," I said. "I do it all the time, just for fun."

DeWayne started to pick up a rag, then shook his head and started for the door again. "I'm not supposed to get my hands dirty. I guess I'll have to let you have all the fun."

"I'll let you play my Nintendo if you'll help," I said.

"I got a Nintendo," he said. "I gotta go now."

"I'll let you hold one of my rats," I said.

"Naw. He might bite me," DeWayne said, moving closer to the door.

"I'll give you a dollar," I said.

"I've got forty-seven dollars in my bank at home," he said. "I'm rich."

That gave me an idea.

I picked up a sugar bowl and started rubbing polish on it, not looking at DeWayne. "That's no money," I said. "I know a way you could get really rich."

I held the sugar bowl up to the light and then rubbed it some more. "Never mind," I said. "I don't guess I want to tell you about it after all."

"What?" DeWayne said, pulling a chair out and sitting down beside me. He put his face up next to mine. "What, J.R.?"

"Well, OK," I said. "Wait here." I handed him the sugar bowl and rag. "I'll be right back."

I ran up to my room and found a magazine with an ad for sea monkeys. "Looky here," I said when I got back downstairs. "You can order some of these real-live sea monkeys. See their little smiley faces? Ain't they cute? Only nine ninety-eight plus shipping and handling. What you could do is you could raise them and sell them to the other kids when school starts. You could make a lot more than forty-seven dollars, I bet."

DeWayne held the ad up and squinted at it.

"I wish I had some," I lied. "But I'm not rich like you are."

"Yeah," DeWayne said. "Can I have this magazine, J.R.?"

"Sure," I said, "just as soon as we finish this silver."

DeWayne was pretty slow and he left a lot of spots on the silver, but it was better than no help at all. After we finished, I gave him the magazine and he went mincing back down the sidewalk.

"Wash your hands, J.R.," Biggie said, coming down the stairs. "I want you to go downtown with me."

I didn't argue on account of I'd rather hang around an antique store than stay around here and have Willie Mae work me like a dog all morning.

3

The town of Job's Crossing is built around a square with the courthouse in the middle. If you come down Elm Street, you'll see the Owl Café on the corner. It is run by Mr. Populus, who is Greek. He makes the best pies in town, but I wouldn't want Willie Mae to hear me say that. On the other end of the block is Handy's House of Hardware, and in between the two is Macon's Dry Goods, where Biggie buys most of her clothes. Mrs. Macon special orders for her on account of Biggie being so small. That's just one side of the square. The statue of Biggie's ancestor, James Royce Wooten, stands on the east side of the courthouse lawn in the shade of a large magnolia tree. Old James Royce is wearing fringed buckskins and a Davy Crockett hat. One hand holds a long rifle while the other shades his eyes as he looks toward Plumley's Rexall across the street. Between Plumley's and the barbershop next-door, you will find some stairs going up. That is where Miss Moseley teaches piano and voice after school and on Saturdays. You do not want to go to

Plumley's from 3:00 to 3:45 on Thursdays, on account of that is the time Mrs. Muckleroy takes her voice lessons. It sounds a lot like Booger when he wants to go outside and nobody will open the door for him. Next to that is the new newspaper office that Mr. H.C. Crouch opened up last year. Now we don't have to get all our news from the Center Point paper. After that, you pass the Piggly Wiggly, where we get all our groceries. Miss Dossie's is on the south side of the square between Itha's House of Hair and Miss Mattie Thripp's tearoom.

"Ummm, smell that magnolia," Biggie said as we crossed the courthouse lawn. "I just love spring in East Texas."

"Biggie," I said, "could we stop in at the drugstore for a milk shake?"

Biggie had stopped at the statue of her ancestor and taken a tissue out of her purse. She was working on a pile of pigeon poop that had landed on James Royce's foot. "You bet," she said, not looking at me. "Soon as we buy that platter. My soul, would you look what Dossie's done to this place."

It was a sight all right. She had painted the front of the store a bright robin's egg blue, with pink trim. And she had a new sign that had been carved out of wood with old-timey letters. The sign read:

DOSSIE'S ANTIQUES
New and Old
(Tanning Salon in Rear!)

"My, oh, my," Biggie said, "looks like Dossie's expanded her business."

We stood for a minute looking through the dust at the things in the window. There was a large bust of an Indian chief carved out of a log, which I mentioned might look good on our front porch, but Biggie didn't think so. She was busy examining the chipped dishes and bent silverware and crooked candlesticks.

"See that platter?" she said. "I do believe it matches the one you broke."

With that, Biggie pushed open the door, and a little bell tinkled as we went in. Miss Dossie stuck her head around a display of antique corncob pipes. She was sitting behind the counter gluing the handle back on a blue teapot. Miss Dossie is tall and slim and very pretty in a grubby kind of way, if you know what I mean. Her hair falls to the middle of her back and is curlier than Willie Mae's. Miss Dossie mostly wears it loose and held back with old-timey combs from her shop. Her earrings brush her shoulders, and her dresses flow almost to the floor.

"Y'all come on in," she said.

I just love that store. There are shelves on each side just crammed full of old magazines like *Life* and *Collier's* and the *Saturday Evening Post*. I really like looking at the funny way people used to dress and wear their hair back then. She has a big box in the corner that is full of old-timey postcards and Christmas cards and Valentines. She even has actual letters people wrote to each other mixed in. In another box are old snapshots. Miss Dossie told me that when somebody dies she just calls up the relatives and tells them she'll buy whatever they don't want out of the dead person's stuff. She said you'd be surprised what people will leave because they don't know it's valuable. She said she once got an entire set of Fiesta Ware that was practically like brand-new.

Biggie walked over and plucked the platter from the window. She brushed it off, then turned it over to look at the mark on the bottom. "How much are you asking for this?" she asked. The platter was cream-colored, with designs all over it in orange and dark blue.

Miss Dossie put on the glasses she was wearing around her neck on a blue velvet ribbon. She squinted at Biggie. "Hold it up so I can see it," she said. "Oh, that there's genuine Staffordshire. I'll have to get a hunnerd and forty-five for that."

"Dossie, it's got 'Canton, Ohio' stamped on the back. I'm not paying that much for this old thing."

Miss Dossie was already bent over the teapot she was gluing. "Whatever melts your butter," she said. "Did y'all hear about old H. C. Crouch? They tell he sent off for one of those Filipino brides."

"Who told you that?" Biggie asked, fingering a vase shaped like a woman's head. "No, don't tell me. Luther Abernathy."

"Naturally," Miss Dossie said. "You don't think old H.C.'s gonna print it up in his newspaper, do you? Luther says they sent H.C. a whole bunch of pictures in a book — like a catalog. Luther said some of the girls were right pretty, but most would have to sneak up on the dipper to get a drink."

"Did the catalog have prices?" I asked.

"I don't think so," Miss Dossie said. "I guess they were all the same. Luther didn't say."

"What if you ordered one and you didn't like her? Could you send her back?"

"That's a real good question, J.R. I'm going to have to ask Luther about that next time he comes in. I'll tell you one thing: I'd sure hate to be that poor Filipino girl that got here and found out she'd been bought by

H.C. That man looks like a frog and talks like a preacher. His mouth reaches from ear to ear, and it don't quit flapping from sunup to sundown."

Biggie picked up the platter again and held it up to the light. "It's chipped on the bottom," she said. "I'll tell you what; I'll give you twenty-five dollars for it. Cash money."

"I'll have to look up my cost on it," Miss Dossie said. "Tell you what. Why don't you-all browse around the shop 'til this glue sets."

I looked up from sniffing the empty perfume bottles grouped on a whatnot shelf. "Can I see the tanning salon?" I asked.

Miss Dossie blew her nose on a lace hankie. "I declare, the hay fever's got me this year. Must be all them mimosa trees." She waved the hankie at me. "Sure, J.R., just go down that hall. I got a massage table back there, too. What I did was I converted the storage room into a holistic health center like they got in Austin and them places." She sneezed. "You ought to let me give you my super-special all-over deep massage, Miss Biggie. You'll feel like a new woman. I guarantee."

Biggie had turned away from the platter and was pulling some old dresser scarves out of a steamer trunk. She held one out in front of her. "This looks just like one my mother used to have. Cut work. You don't see that much anymore. Folks just don't have the time. Too bad it's got ink on it. How much?"

"I generally get forty-five dollars," Miss Dossie said, staring down at her teapot.

"For this old thing?" Biggie asked.

"Oh. No, I can let you have that for seven-fifty. I meant the massage."

"I didn't know you were a massage therapist," Biggie said.

"Oh, yes, ma'am. Certified and everything. I took one of those correspondence courses. They sent me a whole lot of books and diagrams and stuff. I studied up on it and practiced on my dog, Bouncer. When I finished, they sent me a nice certificate suitable for framing." She laughed. "That old pooch got so relaxed he like to slept his life away while I was takin' that course."

I headed toward the back. The narrow hallway was littered with cardboard boxes spilling over with junk, along with some broken chairs and an old sewing machine. I was surprised when I came to the room at the end of the hall, on account of it was fixed up real nice. Miss Dossie had painted the walls light blue. Someone had painted life-size fat ladies dancing around a maypole on one wall. They were all naked except for some floaty ribbons that trailed around them covering their private parts. The concrete floor was painted dark green and was covered with a soft yellow-and-blue rug. A big fake palm tree stood in the corner by the back door. I heard weird soft music coming from a stereo hidden behind some books. The air smelled funny. When I looked to see where the smell was coming from, I saw a china Buddha sitting on a table holding an incense stick between his feet.

Against one wall I could see what I guessed was the massage table. It looked just like those hospital carts only it had a padded hole like a doughnut at one end. The tanning bed was on the opposite wall. It resembled a coffin with a silver lining and a bunch of lights attached to the lid. Shelves at one end of the room held bottles of pills with names like *bee balm* and *evening primrose oil*. The back door that led to the alley had a little ruffledy curtain covering the glass panes.

"J.R.," Biggie called from the hallway, "we have to go!" Biggie was carrying a grocery sack holding the platter.

"How much did the platter cost you?" I asked when we were back on the sidewalk.

Biggie grinned. "We finally settled on thirty-five dollars," she said. "My gracious, look at the time. We'll have to have our milk shake another day. It's lunchtime."

Willie Mae had steaming bowls of white bean soup with ham hocks set out on the kitchen table when we came in. She had made hot-water corn bread and there were homemade peach pickles on the side. For dessert she'd made chocolate dump cake with white icing and red cherries on the top. I had just sopped up the last of my soup with a piece of corn bread and was eyeballing the cake when Willie Mae said, "Miss Biggie, these here are the last of the pickled peaches."

Biggie pointed to her cheeks to show that she had a mouthful of corn bread and couldn't talk. She swallowed, then said, "Well, I sure hate that."

"I could put up some more on Thursday if I had me some good peaches," Willie Mae said.

"It's too early for fresh peaches," Biggie said, cutting herself a piece of cake.

"I reckon not," Rosebud said, cutting a big slab of cake for himself. "They were telling down at the feed store that the Indian peaches are ripe — on account of we had such a mild winter, doncha know. I bet Coye

Sontag's got some he'll sell you."

"Let's go to the farm, Biggie," I said. "I haven't seen Monica since I don't know when."

Biggie had saved the cherry off her cake for last. Now she popped it in her mouth. "I'm too busy to go today."

"Yes, you can, Miss Biggie," Willie Mae said. "If I can get everybody out of the house, I'll have us ready for that meeting in no time. But if y'all stay around here getting in my way, I just don't know. . . ."

"Well . . . ," Biggie said.

"Sure we can, Biggie," I said. "I'll bet Mr. Sontag's got some more of those peas you like. And Mrs. Sontag would like to visit with you, I bet. You know, she gets lonesome out there in the country with nobody to talk to but Monica and Mr. Sontag."

"Well, all right," Biggie said, "but I'm going to have a little nap first. J.R., I want you to help Rosebud wash down the front of the house. We'll leave about three."

Biggie grew up on the farm where Monica and her folks live. She still owns it but lets the Sontags live there for a dollar a year and they give us all the fresh vegetables we can eat. Ten years ago, Mr. Sontag put in a peach orchard. Every summer he sets up a shed beside the road where he sells peaches and other stuff from his garden.

The whole family was sitting in lawn chairs under the shed when Rosebud drove the car up and parked under a sweet gum tree. The shed has a tin roof, and it's held up by two-by-fours. It looks like a good wind would blow it away, but Monica says her daddy set those posts in concrete and it will survive a tornado. Monica has more confidence in her daddy then she ought to is what I think. Bushel baskets were sitting all around the front filled with peas and new potatoes, roasting ears, squash, and peaches. The tables inside the shed were loaded down with smaller baskets filled with tomatoes, some ripe and some green for pickling, okra, peppers, and cucumbers. Mrs. Sontag even had some jars of home-made jams and preserves for sale.

"Y'all got here just in time," said Mrs. Sontag, who is round as an apple and very jolly. She dipped a paper towel in a washtub where they had iced down some cold drinks and wiped her face with it. "We had so many customers this morning, I just this minute got to set and blow awhile."

"Well, Mama, you cain't get no lard if you don't boil the hog," Mr. Sontag said, stuffing a fresh wad of Red Man in his mouth.

"That's right, Coye," Mrs. Sontag said with a grin. "But it wouldn't hurt if you'd help stir the pot once in a while. You've had your butt in that chair since sunup."

Biggie was browsing through the baskets of produce, feeling tomatoes and sniffing cantaloupes. "I hope you didn't sell all the peaches," she said. "Willie Mae has her head set on putting up some peach pickles this week."

"I've got one bushel left," Mrs. Sontag said. "Coye, get up and put these in Miss Biggie's car." She started sacking up cantaloupes. "These cantaloupes are sweet as honey," she said. "Course, we didn't grow um; ours won't be in 'til July. These here were trucked in from the valley." She started loading fat green tomatoes into another sack. "Now, you tell Willie Mae to make you some green tomato relish with these," she said. "There's nothing goes with fried catfish like green tomato relish. Monica, honey, run back to the house and bring some more paper sacks. We've run clean out."

Monica motioned for me to follow, and we climbed under the bob-wire fence and headed across the pasture toward the old gray farmhouse. Monica's dog Buster led the way with his ears back and his tail high.

Monica is my best friend even though she

is a girl. She's small and wiry and can run faster than anybody I know. She has so many freckles that in the summer they run together on her arms so it looks like just one giant freckle. She only has hair on one side of her head on account of being left too close to the fire when she was a baby, but you could hardly tell it today because she'd gone and gotten herself a burr haircut.

"How come you cut off all your hair?" I asked.

"Had to," she said. "That old barn cat gave me ringworm. It's well now. Want to feel my head?" She took my hand and rubbed it on the top of her head. I jerked my hand away.

"It's OK," she said. "I'm well, now. Mama shaved my head and put blue salve on me for a week." She giggled. "You should have seen me, J.R. My head looked like a blue bowling ball. Watch out!"

I stopped where I stood. "Huh?"

"You're standing in a fire ant bed," she said, pointing.

When I looked down, I saw my feet were covered with red ants and they were crawling up my leg. I jumped out of the way and commenced brushing the things off of me. "Ow! One got me! Oh, ouch!"

Monica helped me brush the critters off,

but she was laughing her head off. "You looked like a turkey with his head chopped off, dancing around like that."

"Let's go," I said.

"I saw them ants kill a baby calf once," Monica said. "My daddy says it's because of them we don't see many deer around here anymore."

"Go on!"

"No, really. The mama doe will leave the fawn in a safe place while she goes away to eat, and when she gets back that little feller will be nothin' but a pile of bones."

"Yuk."

"I know. I hate um."

When we got back with the sacks, Biggie and Rosebud were sitting under the shed with the Sontags drinking iced tea from fruit jars.

"See that crow up in the top of that tree?" Monica said. "Watch this." She picked a peach out of a box of culls, wound up, and threw it hard at the bird. She hit him dead on. The crow dropped on the ground like a stone, flopped around scattering feathers for a minute, then took off for a fence post where he sat preening himself. Every few minutes he'd glare at Monica and squawk at her.

Monica flopped down on the ground and

sat with her back to a tree. "You can't hurt them crows," she said with a grin. "They're tougher than a sow's snout."

Rosebud put down his tea and walked over to where we were standing. "Can you do that again?" he asked.

"Sure," Monica said, "but I think I ought to let that old crow rest a minute. He ain't made out of iron."

Rosebud walked over to the trash barrel and pulled out a soda can. He walked over to the fence, which was about fifteen yards away, and put the can on a fence post. "Can you hit this?" he called.

Monica picked up another peach and sent that can flying across her daddy's pea patch.

Next, Rosebud lined up four cans, each on a fence post. Monica knocked them all down quick as hot grease. Rosebud didn't say anything, just went back under the shed and started talking to the Sontags.

After a while, Rosebud and Mr. Sontag loaded up the trunk of Biggie's car with peaches, tomatoes, cantaloupes, and mustard greens.

"That wild plum jelly looks good," Biggie said. "But I don't dare take any home. Willie Mae's right touchy about me buying jelly when she makes it so good herself."

"Well, here," Mrs. Sontag said, going to

the back of the shed. "Take some of these plums. We get them off the wild trees in the woods." She filled a sack with red plums, then grabbed another jar off the shelf. "You gotta try some of Coye's honey, too. It'll go good on Willie Mae's hot biscuits. Oh, wait. . . ." She waddled over to the cooler and pulled out a pound of homemade butter. "You're gonna need some of this, too. And let me sack you up some of these yard eggs. I gathered them fresh this morning."

"Ernestine," Biggie said, "between your good farming and Willie Mae's cooking we'll all be fat as boardinghouse cats. Get in the car, J.R. Willie Mae will have supper ready soon."

I sat in the back wedged between the eggs and tomatoes, which Biggie didn't want to put in the trunk on account of they are fragile. As we pulled out onto the road, I saw Monica chunk another peach at that crow. This time he flew away before she could hit him. Once we got on the road, I asked, "Rosebud, why were you so interested in Monica chunking peaches?"

"She set me to thinkin' about something that happened when I was just a kid, no older than you and Monica," he said.

"Tell it."

Rosebud rolled down the window and lit

up one of his cigars. He held it out the window with his left hand and steered the car with his right. "It was in the summer," he said. " 'Bout this time of year as I recollect. A carnival had come to our town."

"Like the one we had at the Pioneer Days Festival?"

"Hmmm. Something like that. Only this here carnival had sights like you never seen before. They had a elephant with two heads, one facing north and the other south. Ooowee, that was a sight to see. He could walk which-um ever way he chose to without ever needin' to turn around. He was right handy around the carnival — helpin' set up tents and all."

"Golly!"

"But that ain't all. They had a gentleman there who would eat live turtles. He'd just put um in a bowl, sprinkle on a little salt and pepper, and crunch away. He only ate the small turtles. Claimed they had a more delicate flavor — tasted something like roasted hickory nuts. He kept another bowl nearby to spit the shells in."

"You can get salmonella from turtles. Right, Biggie?"

"So I heard," Biggie said.

"Oh, not him. He was a big strappin' feller. Used to tell folks it all come from eatin' turtles. Claimed they was chock-full of vitamins and all like that. Claimed he'd never been sick a day in his life."

"Rosebud," I said. "What's this got to do with Monica chunking peaches?"

Rosebud put on the gas and passed a tractor that was poking along down the road. "I'm getting to that, ain't I?" he said after we were back in our lane. "Along with the carnival and the rides and freaks and such, they had game tents. You know, where you toss a ball at a milk bottle and win a teddy bear."

"Sure, I know," I said. "Like the dunking booth we had at Pioneer Days."

"That's right. Only the places at this here carnival were all rigged — ever' one of um. But the worst one was a place that claimed they'd give you a beautiful doll with a sparkly red dress and long blond hair if you could chunk a ball through a hole about the size of Willie Mae's embroidery hoop. Well, my baby sister Shenestra had her heart set on that doll. She spent all her allowance, not to mention the money she'd been saving in her piggy bank, just to get that doll. It was crooked, doncha know. They had that thing rigged so nobody could ever win."

"How?"

"Mirrors, son. They done it with mirrors.

59

Well, sir, I decided to get my little sis that doll, and I knew in a fair game I could do it."

"But this wasn't a fair game. Right?"

He slowed the car down to let some cows cross the road. "Right. So I had to even the odds. I stood by that tent night after night watching fellers chunk that ball, tryin' to win that doll for their wives and girlfriends. It looked to me like the ball was gonna fly right through the hole, then it ud just bounce away. One night, I was standin' over to the side watching, and just as the Ferris wheel lights fell on a certain spot, I saw what it was. He had stuck a mirror in the hole at an angle so that when you stood in front of it, what looked like the hole wasn't — it was the reflection of the hole."

"Wow! What a gyp!"

"Gyp is right. But I was smarter than them guys. It so happened that there was a tree growin' off to the side of that tent. That gave me an idea. I borrowed a signal lantern off my Uncle Phinus, who was a brakeman for the L.A. & T. Them things put out a powerful light. Then I sent Shenestra up the tree with the lantern. We practiced the night before I planned to win that doll. Shenestra would shine the light, and I'd signal her when it was just exactly right where I could see the hole the way it really was and not reflected in that mirror. Wellsir, the next night I was loaded for bear, doncha know. I waited until a crowd had gathered around that booth, then walked up to take my turn. I paid my money and the man set three balls down in front of me. I nodded to Shenestra up in the tree and wound up to throw. Shenestra shined the light, but just as I let go of the ball she sneezed and the lamp moved off its point. The ball bounced on the floor in front of me. The carnival feller smiled a smug smile. I looked at Shenestra and wound up again. This time, a lady carrying a baby had come up beside me to see the action. Just as I was about to throw, that baby grabbed my arm. I only had one ball to go and couldn't buy no more, on account of I had spent my last dollar on them three balls. Well, Shenestra, she shone the light, and I threw the ball. *Smuck!*" Rosebud hit the steering wheel. "Right through the hole! My baby sister like to cried from happiness when she got her doll, and that carnival feller, well, he lost his smarty-pants grin."

"I don't see what that's got to do with Monica — wait a minute! What's that in the ditch up ahead?"

Biggie craned her neck to look. "There it is, to your right by that sycamore tree. Oh, my stars, Rosebud, stop! Somebody's had a wreck."

Rosebud slowed the car and pulled onto the grass by the side of the road. A car had skidded off the pavement and was turned upside down in the ditch. Rosebud jumped out of the car and ran to the edge of the ditch, then stopped.

He turned and held his hand up like a traffic cop. "Stay back," he said. "The motor's still running. This thing could blow any minute."

"Biggie, look!" I said. "Somebody's in there. I see an arm hanging out the window."

"Looks like Luther Abernathy's old Camaro," Biggie said. "Rosebud, wait!"

But she was too late. Rosebud had scooted down the hill and was racing toward the car. Quicker than hell could scorch a feather, he reached his arm in the window and cut off the engine. Then he did something with his hand inside the car. He looked back up the hill toward Biggie.

"It's that mailman," he said. "And he ain't breathin'."

4

Biggie stood with her hands on her hips and looked all around. Across the road and through a grove of oak trees I could see the roof of a farmhouse. Biggie pointed that way. "I believe that's Hoss Henderson's house," she said. "Looks like it's the nearest, but it's a good little way up there. Oh, well, let's get started." She started back across the ditch and toward the road.

"Miss Biggie, seems to me like it ain't proper to just leave old Luther here all by hisself," Rosebud said, still standing in the ditch.

"I guess you're right," Biggie said. "You're sure he's dead?"

"Oh, yes, ma'am. He done delivered his last 'lectric bill."

"J.R. . . ."

"Not me!" I said.

Rosebud took out a red bandanna handkerchief and wiped his forehead. Then he said, "Y'all go on, Miss Biggie. I'll stay. Just hurry on back now. You hear?"

Biggie was already trotting off down the

road with me at her heels.

The Henderson place set at the top of a hill about half a mile away. The long, curved driveway was covered with powdery white sand that had turned our shoes snow-white when we finally came huffing up to the old unpainted farmhouse that sat creaking in the sun. A large tin shed off to the side held a tractor, a road grader, and a big yellow bull-dozer. When I asked why they were there, Biggie told me Mr. Henderson was a county commissioner and was responsible for maintaining the roads in his precinct.

We found Mrs. Henderson digging in the flower beds beside the wide front porch. She stood up and put her hands on her waist and stretched backward, like she'd been working a long time. I saw she was a slim lady with soft brown hair, damp from sweat as it curled around her face. She bowed her head kind of like she was shy, but her lips were smiling as she walked toward us. Three cow dogs crawled out from under the wood steps and set up an awful racket.

"Hush, dogs," Mrs. Henderson said, brushing her hands on her apron. "Hidy, Miss Biggie. Is this J.R.? Ain't he grown!"

Biggie wiped the sweat off her forehead with her arm and nodded. "Honey, there's been an accident," she said. "We need to use

64

your phone right away."

"Well, come on in," Mrs. Henderson said. "Nobody hurt, I hope. You dogs git, now. No! Leave Miss Biggie alone!"

We followed Mrs. Henderson through the screen door into a wide, cool hall that ran the length of the house. The walls were bare wood, but pictures of old-timey folks in old-timey frames hung on both sides. There was a table up against one wall that was covered with a crocheted tablecloth. It held a vase of plastic flowers. I could see all the way through the house to the back porch. The place smelled like somebody was cooking turnip greens. She led us into a sitting room on the right. Mr. Henderson was watching Geraldo on TV. When he saw Biggie, he flipped up his Lazy Boy and commenced putting on his big old work shoes.

"Don't bother getting up, Hoss," Biggie said. "Luther Abernathy's car turned over in the ditch, and he's in it. Looks like he's dead. I need to call Butch and have him bring the ambulance."

While Biggie was making her call, I strolled over to the mantle where Mrs. Henderson had put her family pictures. I saw a real old-timey picture of a bride and groom, a picture of a girl in a basketball uniform who looked a good bit like Mr.

65

Henderson, and a big picture of a dead woman laid out in her casket with flowers all around. She was holding a Bible in her hands. Mrs. Henderson told me that was the only picture she had of her poor old mama, who had worked all her life chopping cotton over in Rains County. I was about to ask about the girl in the basketball uniform when Biggie came back into the room.

"Butch will be right on out," she said. "We'd better get back."

"It's a downright dirty-dog shame, is what it is," Mr. Henderson said, pulling the bib of his overalls over his belly and buckling just one of the straps. "Luther was slow as molasses in January, but I always said he had a good heart. Didn't I always say that, honey?"

Mrs. Henderson beamed at her husband. "You sure did," she said. "Ever' time he'd come out here bringing our mail along with all the news in town, Hoss would say, 'That Luther, he's a humdinger of a mailman.'"

"Are they anything we can do?" Mr. Henderson asked.

Just then, the phone rang. Mrs. Henderson answered and came back saying it was for Biggie.

After listening a minute, Biggie said, "What do you mean, we don't have a wrecker, Butch? We have to have the wrecker. Luther's car is upside-down in the ditch, and he's pinned. . . ."

She listened some more.

"You mean to tell me Aubrey Dunbar's taken his wife to Tyler shopping in the *wrecker?* OK. . . . OK. . . . Well, get out here as fast as you can with the ambulance. And bring Doc Potter with you. OK. . . . Yes. . . . Well, I'm sure they're very pretty. . . . Yes. . . . Yes. Butch, I've got to go. We've got a dead man to deal with! Yes, good-bye. . . . No, I can't talk now. . . . No. Good-bye."

Biggie turned to Mr. Henderson. "Honey, maybe there is something you can do," she said. "Do you think one of those big machines you've got would pull that car out of the ditch?"

"You betcha," Mr. Henderson said. "Lemme just get my tractor and a trace chain. Y'all want to ride with me?"

Biggie was already headed out the door. "We'll meet you," she said. "Turn left out of your drive. It's about half a mile — toward town."

When we got back, Rosebud was sitting on the grass. He had a pile of letters beside him.

"Looks like he musta been deliverin' his rural route when he piled up his car," he said. "I found this mail in the backseat."

"Why don't you put it in our car?" Biggie said. "We can drop it off at the post office when we get back to town. Oh, here comes Hoss."

Mr. Henderson came bouncing up on his tractor, which was red and had a big yellow umbrella with DEKALB CORN printed in black letters across the top. He backed the tractor up to the ditch and tossed a heavy chain with hooks on both ends to the ground. Rosebud picked up one end and hooked it to the bumper of Luther's car, then hooked the other end to the back of the tractor.

"Pull her slow," he called, "or she'll flip on you!" He turned to Biggie. "Miss Biggie, I reckon you and J.R. better get out by the side of the road and wave the traffic on by."

I didn't expect to see much traffic, but I walked a few yards toward town and stood next to the road in case any cars happened to come by. Biggie took the other side. Just as I saw the back end of Luther's car creeping up over the side of the ditch, a car appeared over the next hill coming lickety-split. Mr. Henderson's tractor was almost to the yellow line in the middle of the road. I waved my arms and jumped up and down, but that car didn't slow down one bit. If any-thing, the driver gave it more gas. It went flying past the tractor, kicking up dirt on the other side of the road. As it passed, I saw it was pulling a metallic blue bass boat.

"Gawd dawg!" Rosebud said, scratching his head. "Who was that?"

"I don't know who it was," I said, "but that was Mr. Matkin's bass boat. I see it at the lake all the time."

"Matkin," Biggie said. "I don't know any Matkins around here. What do you know about him?"

I was glad to be able to tell Biggie something she didn't already know. "Remember when we had the middle school picnic out at the lake? Well, we were swimming in the roped-off area when this big old blue boat came racing by. It almost ran over Binky Wells, who wasn't doing a thing but floating on his back. He swallowed so much water, he had to throw up all afternoon. The eighth-grade teacher, Mrs. Fuller, said they were new people from the city. They built a new house out close to Mrs. Fuller. That's how she knew whose boat it was."

"Listen," Biggie said. "I hear Butch coming with the ambulance."

By that time, Mr. Henderson had the car right-side-up and on the shoulder of the road. I peeped in the window before Biggie could stop me, then turned around and was sick on the grass. Luther had been shaken up quite a bit from being dragged, and his head was flopped sideways across his chest like a rag doll. Blood was coming out of his mouth and ears.

The ambulance siren whined louder and louder until, finally, Butch screeched to a stop, barely missing Luther's car. He jumped out and ran over to look at Luther.

"Ooh, yuk!" he said. "Why didn't you say he was all bloody? I feel faint. I faint at the sight of blood."

"Butch, go turn off that siren," Biggie said. "And help the doctor out of the car. He seems to be having trouble."

"Oh, yeah," Butch said. "That door's temperamental sometimes. You have to hold your mouth just right, or it won't open."

While Butch helped the doctor, I couldn't help it. I snuck one more look at Luther. I wish I hadn't. One of his dead eyes was staring right at me. I got behind Biggie.

Doc Potter came over to the car carrying his little black bag, stepping high over the Johnson grass. The doc is a short man with wide hips like a woman. His skin is white as a biscuit, and his hair is the color of river mud, brownish-gray, and wispy. Today the wind was blowing it all over the place. He looked in the window at Luther.

"Hmmm," he said, "must have had a heart attack while driving. Happens all the time. You never know when the old ticker's going to go."

Biggie rolled her eyes. "Aren't you going to examine him?" she asked.

"I suppose I must," the doctor said, "but it's his heart. I can always tell. See his ashen color?"

"He's dead, Avery," Biggie said. "Of course he's pale."

"Oh, well," the doctor said. "Get him out of the car so I can look him over."

Rosebud and Butch went back to the ambulance and pulled a stretcher out of the back while Mr. Henderson walked around Luther's car.

"How we gonna get him outta there, Miss Biggie?" he asked. "That there door's smashed in right smart."

"We'll have to call in the Jaws of Life," I said.

"J.R., this is Kemp County," Biggie said. "We don't have any Jaws of Life. You've been watching too much TV."

"I know something might work," Mr. Henderson said. "I could go get my welding rig. I could cut that door off with my cutting torch."

"Do it then," Biggie said.

71

It was pitch-dark before we rolled back into town. When they finally got Luther laid out on the stretcher, Doc kept insisting he'd died of a heart attack but did admit that he had a right smart blow to the head in the bargain. Truth of the matter was, the back of his head was bashed flat. That's where a lot of that blood was coming from.

At the supper table, we told Willie Mae all about it.

"I saw him, Willie Mae," I said. "He had blood all over him. They had to take his body over to Center Point, on account of we don't have an undertaker anymore since Monk Carter got killed. Can I have some more ham and another biscuit?"

Willie Mae speared a slice of country ham on my plate and buttered a biscuit for me. "Pore little young'un," she said.

"Huh?" I said.

"Never mind. Miss Biggie, did you say y'all found a mess of mail in his car?"

"I better go get it," Rosebud said. "We can't leave the U.S. Mail out there all night."

"Why don't I just ride my bike down to the corner and drop it in the mailbox?" I asked.

Biggie was spreading butter on a biscuit.

"No," she said. "There's nobody to pick it up now that Luther's gone. I want to take it to the post office. While I'm there, I want to give that postmaster a piece of advice about hiring. We need a more *discreet* person to take Luther's place." She yawned. "I feel like I could sleep until noon tomorrow."

Willie Mae got up and went to refill the gravy bowl. "I reckon you must of forgot about your meetin'," she said.

"You're right," Biggie said. "I'd forgotten all about it. Well, we'll have to deal with the mail after the Daughters leave."

Willie Mae went into the kitchen and brought out a poppy seed cake with lemon frosting. As she sliced it, she asked, "Did anybody think about notifyin' the poor man's family?"

"I don't think Luther's got any family around here," Biggie said. "I guess we'd better go over to his house and see what we can find out. Honey, pass me some more gravy." She poured redeye gravy over a biscuit and ate it before she spoke again. "Now I'm ready for some cake. Why hasn't Paul and Silas called? I left a message on his answering machine the minute we got home."

Paul and Silas is our cousin from Tennessee that Biggie roped into being police chief on account of, at the time, the only policeman we had was Butch, who everyone said was not suited for the job. Paul and Silas has two names from the Bible on account of his mama always wanted him to grow up to be a preacher.

"I don't think Paul and Silas likes his job much," I said. "He told me if the highway patrol ran in one more drunk to vomit all over his nice clean jail cell, he was going to walk right out of there."

5

The Daughters started arriving at eleven the next morning.

I sat on the stair landing and watched as they came trooping in the front door. First, Mrs. Muckleroy and Mrs. Moody. Mrs. Muckleroy must have been wearing one of her new wigs. It was reddish blond, all piled on top with little curls hanging down. Mrs. Moody had on a bright pink pantsuit, and her hair was fuzzy around her face. She had one round circle of pink rouge on each cheek.

Next came Miss Julia Lockhart, who writes a weekly column for our newspaper, and Miss Lonie Fulkerson, who is very nice but hard to understand because she is tongue-tied. She looked like she had just gotten up from her nap and forgotten to comb her hair. It was all flat on one side. Miss Lonie spotted me and waved her hankie. I was worried that she was about to come over and hug me, but just that minute Biggie came walking out of the living room to greet them. She was wearing a blue denim skirt and a white blouse, with a red scarf around her neck. She had on her white tennis shoes.

"Come on in," she said, waving them in with the teapot she was carrying. "Have a seat while I take this back to the kitchen. Who wants tea, and who wants Willie Mae's dewberry wine?"

"Ooh, I juth love Willie Mae's homemade wine," Miss Lonie squealed.

Miss Julia and Mrs. Moody said they'd take wine, too.

Mrs. Muckleroy said she'd just have tea. "I know you think a lot of Willie Mae's cooking, Biggie," she said, "but I remember feeling quite odd after having refreshments at your home last year."

"Suit yourself, honey," Biggie said, disappearing back into the kitchen.

Pretty soon she came back. Willie Mae followed pushing a tea cart that held a carafe of wine, the tea stuff, and silver platters piled high with stuffed celery, cheese straws, and Cajun-roasted pecan halves.

While Willie Mae passed out the refreshments, another group of ladies came in led by Miss Mattie Thripp, who owns Mattie's Tea Room. Miss Mattie was wearing a floaty dress with big yellow roses all over it. She had a yellow ribbon in her frizzy blue hair.

"Girls," Miss Mattie said in a loud voice, "I want to introduce y'all to Twyla Matkin. She's got her papers all ready to send in to the state board, and when she's approved she wants to petition to become a member of our chapter."

Once they were seated, they all started asking the new lady questions.

"Where you from, honey?"

"Muleshoe," she said, raising a cheese straw to her mouth.

"That's West Texas," Miss Julia said with a nod. "My daddy's people came from around there. Did you ever know any Larsons?"

"Ummm," Mrs. Matkins said. "I don't —"

"How come you didn't join the Daughters out there?" Mrs. Muckleroy asked.

Mrs. Matkin was still trying to get a bite of that cheese straw but moved it from her mouth to answer. "I don't think they had a chapter out there," she said.

"Where'd you go to school?"

"Texas Tech."

"Were you in a sorority?"

"Zeta."

"Where do y'all live, sweet?"

"We built out on the lake," Mrs. Matkin said, cramming the cheese straw into her mouth, chewing fast, and taking a big swig

77

of tea. She set down her cup. "My husband loves the water. I declare, he'd rather bass-fish than eat."

Biggie looked up from the minutes of the last meeting she'd been studying. "Does he own a blue bass boat?" she asked.

"Why, yes," Mrs. Matkin said, dabbing her face with a lace hankie. "Jim Bob is a champion bass fisherman. I declare, every weekend it seems like he's gone to some tournament or other."

"Hmm," Biggie said. "Well, let's get all our visiting done before lunch. After lunch, we'll have our business meeting. More wine anyone?"

"Ooh, yeth," Miss Lonie said. "I juth can't get enough of Willie Mae'th dewberry wine."

Three more ladies held their glasses out, and Biggie poured another round.

"Does anyone notice anything different about me?" Mrs. Muckleroy asked with a smirk.

Mrs. Crews, my old second-grade teacher, was talking to the new lady. She turned and looked at Mrs. Muckleroy. "I do, sugar," she said. "You're wearing one of that dead woman's wigs."

Mrs. Muckleroy turned redder than a baboon's butt. "Humph!" she said. "One of these days, that Luther's going to go too . . . oh, my soul . . . I almost forgot. Luther's dead!"

"No need to feel bad, Ruby," Biggie said. "We all know Luther told everything he knew and some he didn't know. Him being dead isn't going to change that."

"Biggie found him," Mrs. Moody said. "In his car."

"Tell us about it," Miss Julia said, taking a little notebook out of her pocket. "I need the facts for the paper."

"Not much to tell," Biggie said. "He must have hit his head when his car went off the road."

By this time, I had moved off the stairs and was sitting on the floor behind the settee.

"I was there," I said. "Blood was all over the place."

The new lady, Mrs. Matkin, started fanning herself with her handkerchief. "Mrs. Weatherford," she said, "may I use your rest room?"

"Call me Biggie," Biggie said. "Everybody does. It's down the hall and to your right."

As soon as the door to the bathroom closed, Mrs. Scroggins leaned in close to the others. "I heard she orders from that home shopping channel on teevee," she said. "All the time. Then she hides the stuff from her husband."

"I heard her husband was tight as wall-paper," Miss Mattie said.

"Luther told me she's got things hid all over the house and the little shed they've got out back," Mrs. Scroggins said. She glanced at the door to be sure Mrs. Matkin wasn't coming back. "She told Luther never to stop at her house if her husband's truck was parked out front."

"So she could grab all the bills before *he* saw them?" Mrs. Crews asked.

"Of course, Myrtyce," Mrs. Muckleroy said, "that's not the question. The question is, do we want a person like that in our chapter? I'm just asking."

"I with I had lot'th of money," Miss Lonie said. "They have thum really nice thingth on that home thopping channel. I thaw where they had a genuine diamond ring for only twenty-nine ninety-five."

"That's not the point, Lonie," Mrs. Moody said. "That point is: Is that any way for a member of the James Royce Wooten Chapter of the DRT to be acting? Hiding things from her husband and all?"

"It's a disease," Miss Mattie said, "like gambling. I saw it on *Oprah*. Uh-oh, quiet, everybody. Here she comes."

"My hair's a mess," Mrs. Scroggins said real fast as Mrs. Matkin came back in the room. "Ever since Hazelle down at the beauty shop got picked to sing alto in that gospel quartet, she hasn't been worth snuff. I declare, if she doesn't quit singing 'Washed in the Blood of the Lamb' while she's shampooing my hair, I'm going to —"

Just then, Willie Mae stuck her head in the door. "Lunch is getting cold," she said.

Card tables had been set up in the sunroom for the ladies. I ate in the kitchen with Willie Mae and Rosebud. We had fruit salad and cream of avocado soup and little bitty finger sandwiches that you had to eat about a dozen of to get full.

After lunch, Willie Mae made me clear off the card tables while the ladies had their meeting. Biggie stood up and tapped her glass with her spoon.

"As you all know," she said, "the Lions Club has kindly deeded a portion of their campground out on the lake to the DRT for the purpose of holding special events. The only trouble is the land is low, and ankle-deep in water in some places."

"Well, my land, we don't want to get eaten up by mosquitoes!" Miss Mattie said.

"That's probably why they gave it to us," Miss Julia said. "What it is, is nothing but a swamp."

"Thill," Miss Lonie said, "it'th near the

lake and hath lot'th of big tree'th."

"I used to ride horses there as a girl," Biggie said. "There's a creek on the property, only now it's filled with trash. Folks have used it for a dump for the Lord knows how long. What I'm thinking is we could dredge out the creek, use the trash for fill, and haul in topsoil to cover the trash. That way, we raise the level of the land and have a nice creek to boot."

Mrs. Crews raised her hand, and Biggie nodded at her.

"As treasurer of this organization," she said, "I feel it's my duty to inform y'all that we now have exactly thirty-two ninety-one in our checking account. We have one outstanding bill: we owe Populus nineteen forty-five for our spring charity: *Pies for the Needy.*"

"Well," Mrs. Scroggins said, "that's that. We can't even pay taxes on the place."

"We got gypped," someone said.

"Let's deed it right back to them," said Mrs. Crews.

"Now, girls," Biggie said. "Are we Daughters or not? Let's put our thinking caps on and figure a way out of this. The chair entertains suggestions from the floor."

"How about asking Hoss Henderson to do the work with his county equipment?"

Miss Mattie said. "Then it wouldn't cost us a thing."

"Won't work," Miss Julia said. "He can't use that equipment for anything but county roads. It's the law."

"Any other suggestions?" Biggie asked. Nobody raised their hands, so she continued. "I propose we have a fund-raiser — and I've got an idea already. We'll have a patriotic rally on July Fourth. I know State Sen. F. L. Lefty Lovelace. He's from Wills Point, you know. Well, we can have him come down and be our celebrity guest."

"We could have an essay contest for the schoolchildren," Mrs. Crews suggested, "on some subject pertaining to the history of Kemp County. The winner could read his or her essay at the rally. That would bring out all the parents."

"We could sell barbecue plates," Mrs. Moody said.

"And cold beer," said another.

"No beer," Biggie said. "The Baptists and Church of Christ would boycott us. We can have soft drinks and Snow-Kones."

"How about a dance?" somebody said.

That's the last I heard on account of I got bored and went upstairs to play video games until the meeting was over. After about an hour, I heard the ladies saying good-bye at the door. A little later, Biggie came up and poked her head in my room.

"I feel like I've been chewed up, spit out, and stepped on," she said. "I think I'll take a little nap."

"Biggie," I said, "did you forget Luther's mail?"

"Sure did!" Biggie said. "The nap will have to wait. Give me a few minutes to change, and we'll drive down to the post office."

The post office is one block off the square on Jefferson Street. It's a red brick building with white trim on the doors and windows. It has slanted cement things beside the steps that I used to slide down when I was a little kid. Today there was a black wreath on the door. Biggie walked to the door marked: POSTMASTER and walked in without knocking. Mr. Florence, the postmaster, had his feet on his desk. He was drinking a cup of coffee and reading a magazine. When he saw Biggie, he dropped his feet and put the magazine on a big pile on his desk. I figured he must be reading everybody's magazines before they got put in the boxes. Mr. Florence has a head shaped like a bullet. He's bald on top with a little gray fringe all around. He has little bitty blue eyes and is very neat. His shoes shine like mirrors, and his uniform pants have creases like knife blades. He told me once he learned to dress by being a marine during the Korean War.

"Afternoon, Miss Biggie," he said. "Shame about Luther. Good man. Hard to replace."

When Mr. Florence talks, it sounds like a gun going off.

"We brought Luther's mail," Biggie said, putting the sackful of mail on Mr. Florence's desk. "Had a chance to think about a replacement?"

"Have to follow postal service procedures," he barked. "Post the job opening. Interview applicants."

"Well, this time I hope you'll hire someone who knows how to keep a rein on his tongue," Biggie said.

Mr. Florence nodded. "Point taken," he said. "Any suggestions?"

"Not at the moment," Biggie said, "but I'll give it some thought."

Mr. Florence picked up a candy jar from the shelf behind him. "Lemon drop?" he asked.

I took one, but Biggie shook her head and asked for Luther's address.

"He lives right near here — just off Willow Street, in one of those little houses near the park," Mr. Florence said. "It's the red one with white shutters."

"We can walk over there," Biggie said. "It's just across the street."

We crossed the street and walked half a block until we came to Luther's house. It was one of three little houses sitting on a huge lot covered with trees. The sidewalk leading to the house was all bumpy and cracked where the tree roots had grown under and pushed up the concrete.

"Biggie, don't you reckon the door's locked? How we going to get in?"

Biggie had already stepped up on the little concrete porch and lifted the doormat. Sure enough, there lay a shiny brass key. Biggie stuck it into the keyhole and pushed open the door. It was light inside on account of Luther didn't have any drapes on the windows, only some raggedy shades that were rolled all the way to the top. The floor was covered with green linoleum, and the walls were covered with faded flowery paper. The only furniture in the room were an old leather sofa and a desk pushed up against the window wall. Biggie went straight to the desk and started going through the drawers while I walked into the kitchen. It had a row of white metal cabinets with a sink in the middle along the back wall. The sink was full of gray dishwater and piled high with dirty dishes. Islands of hardened grease floated on top of the water. A window over the sink overlooked the backyard. Next to that was a torn screen door that led to the backyard. An old-timey chrome table with a yellow plastic top sat next to the door. The one chair matched the table and had a three-cornered rip in the seat with dirty cotton sticking out. Hanging on the wall over the table was a black telephone, and beside it was a closed door. When I peeked in the refrigerator, I could see why Luther was so skinny. There was nothing there but a quart of buttermilk, half a dozen eggs, and a sack from the Eazee Freeze. It held a half-eaten cheeseburger. Just as I was about to open the meat drawer, I heard something. It was coming from the next room and sounded like a baby crying. I slammed the fridge door and went to get Biggie. She was looking through a metal box on top of the desk.

"Biggie," I said.

"Nothing here," she said. "Did you find anything in the kitchen?"

"No'm," I said. "Biggie, there's somebody else in this house besides us."

Biggie got to her feet. "Where?"

"In the bedroom, I guess. There's a door in here." I led Biggie back to the kitchen and pointed to the closed door.

Just then, I heard it cry again. This time, there was no mistaking that sound. "Biggie! It's a puppy!"

Biggie pushed open the door, and sure enough, a little black-and-white puppy came crawling out from under the bed and ran to us, wagging his tail and crying as he came. When I picked him up, he wriggled as close to me as he could get, then peed on my hands. I hugged him closer on account of I figured he had a right to be excited and glad to see us, seeing as how he'd been left all alone for two days.

"Poor fellow," Biggie said, stroking his bumpy little head. "Give him some water J.R." While I did that, Biggie went to the nightstand beside the bed and pulled out the drawer. "Nothing here but a nasal spray and a paperback western," she said. "Well, bring the puppy along. We'll pick up some dog food on the way home."

After supper, while Biggie and Willie Mae watched *Wheel of Fortune*, I was sitting on the floor playing with the puppy when I thought of something. "Biggie," I said, "what about Butch?"

"What *about* Butch?" she asked, not taking her eyes off the screen.

"You said you were going to think about

finding a new mailman."

"*Camp David!*" Biggie hollered.

"Huh?"

"Camp David," she said to the television set. "You've got the *c* and the *p* and *v*. Ask for a *d,* you moron!"

"Humph!" Willie Mae said.

I picked up the puppy and started up the stairs to my room. "I'm keeping him," I said. "And I'm calling him Bingo — like in the song."

Biggie and Willie Mae weren't listening. Pat had just given the wheel a final spin, and it had landed on $10,000.

6

The next morning at breakfast, I brought up the subject of my new baseball mitt again.

"You don't need no new mitt," Rosebud said. "You need to get you some neat's-foot oil and rub down the pocket of your old mitt."

"Can I have it ready before the tournament on Saturday?" I asked.

Rosebud smeared pear honey on a biscuit. "Course," he said, "but you'll have to work hard if you do. Takes elbow grease to condition a glove. Pass that butter over here."

I shoved the butter dish toward Rosebud. "You reckon they'll have a bunch of people there, Rosebud? At the tournament, I mean?"

"There's six towns gonna take part," he said. "I reckon there'll be a whole raft of people — what with the mommas and daddies and all." He grinned and shook his head. "Sure hope they don't have Butch parkin' cars that night."

Biggie looked up from the newspaper she was reading. "Why?" she asked.

Rosebud looked at Biggie. "Well'um," he said, "far be it from me to speak ill of your relatives, but I reckon that Paul and Silas ain't exactly *thrown* himself into the job of bein' police chief."

"Yeah," I said. "He wanted to go out on a date with old Meredith Michelle Muckleroy, so he sent Butch down to direct the car parking at our last game."

Biggie stirred sugar into her coffee. "What's wrong with that?" she asked. "The way people park in this town, it's a wonder we don't have more fender benders than we do."

"Wouldn't have been nothin' wrong with it if he'd of just lined the cars up as they came in," Rosebud said. "It's the way he done it."

"Yeah," I said. "You weren't there that night, Biggie. It was a real mess."

"I remember," Biggie said. "I had that bad sunburn from fishing so long that day and had to miss your game."

Rosebud speared a big piece of Harvey and slid another fried egg onto his plate. "Well, be glad you weren't there," he said. "Butch taken a notion it would *look* better if all the red cars were parked in one row, the blue cars in another, then the whites, the browns, and on like that. Miss Biggie, it was the dernedest mess you ever saw. Folks were honkin' and hollerin'. I had to break up a fistfight between Mr. Handy and Arthur Lee Hooten over whether Mr. Handy's car belonged in the blue row or the green row."

"My goodness," Biggie said. "I guess I'd better have a word with Paul and Silas."

"Biggie," I said after breakfast. "Rosebud says I have to get some neat's-foot oil to condition my mitt. Where do you reckon we could get some?"

"I expect Bertram Handy sells that at the hardware store," she said. "We'll drop by there this morning. Go get washed up."

"I was gonna wash the car this morning," Rosebud said.

"Fine," Biggie said. "It's a nice day for a walk."

The sky was blue, and a nice breeze ruffled Biggie's hair as we strolled down Elm Street toward the square. Redbud blossoms were falling out of the trees and squishing under our feet as we walked. Spring doesn't last hardly a minute in East Texas, but while it's going on it sure makes a person feel good.

The hardware store sits on the far end of the street from the Owl Café, next to the dry goods store. It is the only store downtown that hasn't ever been fixed up one bit. Biggie says it still looks the same way it did when she was a girl — and it was old then. The counters are all wood with glass on the tops and front for display, and they're chock-full of interesting stuff like pocketknives with pearl handles all spread out next to a box of red-and-white fishing bobbers. There are paintbrushes and glue and Zippo lighters and key rings and yardsticks all lined up real neat on account of Mrs. Handy comes down once a week and straightens things up. One end of the counter holds the old-timey cash register, while the other holds a spool of rope that you can buy by the yard and Mr. Handy will cut off for you. Mr. Handy sells a lot of rope on account of in the summer there's always somebody that's got to put up a new rope swing in their backyard. In front of the counter are kegs holding nails of all sizes and shapes, and the shelves behind the counter hold cans of paint in any color a person could ever want. We found Mr. Handy sitting at a table in the back of the store playing dominoes with some other men. They all stood up when Biggie came in.

"Seat yourselves, boys," Biggie said. "Never let it be said that Biggie Weatherford interrupted an important game of dominoes. Just show us where the neat's-foot oil is and you can just put it on my bill."

"Right over there next to the udder balm," Mr. Handy said.

The men all sat back down, and Mr. Norman Thripp commenced mixing the dominoes.

"Matter of fact, Biggie," Mr. Handy said, raising his voice over the clack of the dominoes, "we were just talking about you. Norman here has suggested that it's a dog-gone shame Luther Abernathy met such an untimely death."

"I agree," Biggie said, "but I don't see what that's got to do with me." She reached into the pile of dominoes in the middle of the table and pulled out a hand for herself. "I used to be pretty good at this game," she said.

I pulled up a stool to watch. The men around the table were: Mr. Oterwald, a retired railroad man; Mr. Sloan, who owns the feed store; Mr. Cloyd Whisenant, who walks funny from drinking bad whiskey when he was young; and Norman Thripp, who is married to Miss Mattie and helps out at her tearoom.

"What we was thinking," Mr. Whisenant said, "was wouldn't it be nice if the town bought him a tombstone, or some such thing?"

"Not a tombstone, Cloyd," Mr. Oterwald said. "Luther was a war veteran. The gov'ment'll buy his marker."

"Who says?" Mr. Sloan asked.

"They bought one for my Uncle Clifton," Mr. Oterwald said. "He was in the First World War, doncha know. The VA done it. They sent a nice flag to go on his coffin, too."

"You know, Biggie," Mr. Thripp said, "poor Luther didn't have kith nor kin."

"I heard he had a mama," Biggie said.

"He did — does," Mr. Thripp said, "but she's in the state hospital, thinks she's a duck. Won't eat anything but corn. When it rains, they have to watch her real good or she'll go outside and sit in a puddle. Luther told me all about it one day."

"Sad," Mr. Handy said. "Maybe we could erect a plaque with his name on it. Something in bronze with a nice saying like '*Well done, good and faithful servant.*'"

"That's not a bad idea, Bertram," Biggie said, slapping a double six out on the table. "Maybe we might do something in conjunction with our Fourth of July celebration and fund-raiser. How were you planning to pay for this tribute? Take up a collection among yourselves?"

The men all got real interested in their dominoes.

"Well?" Biggie said. "Plaques cost money, you know."

"I don't know about taking a collection, Biggie," Mr. Thripp said. "Things are mighty tight right now."

The men all nodded.

"Me and Dymple, we just live on our Social Security," Mr. Whisenant said. "That and what she makes down at the school cafeteria."

"I've got an idea," Biggie said. "How about if we plant a tree for Luther in the park? We could have Senator Lovelace make the dedication speech while he's in town."

The men all thought that was a fine idea and started right in arguing about what kind of tree to plant. Mr. Handy was all for a live oak, but Mr. Thripp said they grow too slow.

"How about a nice cottonwood?" he asked.

"Cottonwood's a trash tree," Mr. Oterwald said. "They'll drop that derned cotton all over your food when you go to the park for a picnic. How about a nice mimosa?"

"Excellent," Biggie said, shoving her last domino to the middle of the table. "Looks like I win. Come, J.R.; I want to stop by and see Paul and Silas before lunch."

We found Paul and Silas sitting on a bench in front of the courthouse talking to Floyd and Boyd Vanderslice, the twin paperhangers. They wore twin white overalls and white painters' caps.

"Mornin', Miss Biggie," Floyd said.

"Mornin', J. R.," Boyd said.

"How you . . . ," Floyd said.

"Doin'?" Boyd said.

"Right as rain," Biggie said. "I thought you boys were working on Kathy Lee Blakely's lake house this week."

Floyd looked at his watch. "My gracious, Boyd," he said. "We better get on out there."

"You're right, Brother," Boyd said, "but first, you reckon we ought to ask Miss Biggie's advice on what you and me been . . ."

"Discussing?" Floyd said. "Why don't you go ahead and ask her?"

Boyd turned red. "Well'um, you see, it's this way. Me and Floyd here are sufferin' from what you might call *burnout*."

"That's right," Floyd said. "We seen a story on one of them magazine shows on the teevee. A lot of folks don't realize how stressful paperhangin' can . . ."

"Be," Boyd said.

"So, what we was thinkin'," Floyd said, "was maybe me and Boyd could put in for Luther's job as mail carrier. Shoot, there's two of us. We'd get the mail passed out in half the time."

Biggie hid a grin with her hand. "You'll have to talk to Ed Florence down at the post office," she said. "Right now, you'd better get on out to Kathy Lee's place. I need to have a word with Paul and Silas." She patted Paul and Silas on the shoulder. "Come on — I'll buy you a cup of coffee at the Owl."

After we took a seat in a booth, Mr. Populus came over to take our order. "Peenopple pie straight out of the oven," he said. "Homemade vanilla ice cream on top of."

"I'll go for that," Biggie said.

"Me, too!" I said.

Paul and Silas just asked for a dish of ice cream.

"What's this I hear about you letting Butch park cars at the Little League game?" Biggie asked.

Paul and Silas blushed bright red. "I heard it was a disaster," he said. "I'm sorry, Cousin Biggie. I guess my heart's just not in law enforcement."

"It's not your heart you need to use," Biggie said sternly. "It's your head — and there's never been a Wooten who didn't have a fine head on his shoulders."

"Yes, ma'am," he said. "Well, sometimes I wonder if mine's screwed on right." He brightened. "Still," he said, "there is a matter I've been intending to bring to your attention."

"Shoot," Biggie said.

"Well, upon perusing the file of the accident of our unfortunate mailman, I found some aspects that just don't add up."

"How?" Biggie asked.

"It's the accident report," he said. "It states that Luther died of injuries sustained in the wreck. But, Cousin Biggie, how did he get the *back* of his head crushed? The impact would have propelled him forward so that the *front* of his head should have taken the blow."

"You're right!" Biggie said. "I always knew you had the Wooten brains. Well, now you have something to investigate, don't you? Oh, good, here's Populus with our pie. Dig in, everybody."

7

The next morning, I found Biggie sitting at her desk wearing her fuzzy robe and slippers. She was writing a letter.

"Biggie," I said, just to make conversation, "how come you didn't get all excited when Paul and Silas told you about Luther? I thought you liked mysteries and stuff."

Biggie put down her pen and looked at me. "Well, honey," she said, "Paul and Silas is pretty new at police work. I thought I'd just give him the chance to do this on his own." She picked up a bottle of Jergen's lotion and started rubbing it on her hands. "I'll be standing by if he needs me."

"I bet me and you could solve that case in two days or less. Huh, Biggie?"

Biggie was staring at the paper in front of her and frowning.

"Biggie, when we *are* solving a mystery, who do you think's the best helper, me or Rosebud?"

"Um-humm."

"Biggie! I was talking to you. I said who —"

"J.R., will you please stop asking questions? I can't concentrate."

I sat down at Biggie's dresser and started rearranging all her little bottles and jars. "Biggie, did you know you have three bottles of Olay oil? How come you have to have three bottles of the same stuff?"

Biggie didn't answer.

"Who you writin' to?"

Biggie put down her pen and commenced talking to me real slow. "J.R., I am writing to State Sen. Lefty Lovelace. I am inviting him to come here for a visit so he can get to know our town before the Fourth of July celebration, and I'm having a hard time concentrating with you asking all these silly questions."

"Yes'm."

"Why don't you go outside? It's a beautiful day."

"There's nothin' to do."

"Then go help Rosebud wash the car."

"He's finished already."

"Then get the broom and sweep the front porch and sidewalk."

"Oh, yeah," I said. "I just remembered. I have to rub neat's-foot oil on my mitt before practice this afternoon."

"Then, for the love of Lady Bird, go do it!"

I was thinking I might like to visit Paul and Silas, so I put my glove and neat's-foot oil in a grocery sack, hung it on my handlebars, and rode my bike down to the police station, which is on the south side of the square next to Itha's House of Hair. I found Paul and Silas sitting at his desk pawing through files and talking to Butch.

"Too bad you're not my size," Butch was saying. "I've got some real nice uniforms I don't need anymore. No, honey, don't file that there. That goes under *P* for 'pigeon.'"

Butch was helping Paul and Silas get organized on account of he used to be our police chief. I'll tell you a secret: he wasn't very good at it.

Paul and Silas stared at the paper he was holding. *"P?"* he said. "But it's a bill for steel wool and Mr. Clean. I thought it should go under *C* for 'cleaning supplies.'"

Butch crossed his legs and looked down at his green-sequined tennis shoe. "That's all right, honey," he said. "You'll learn. See, I bought that cleaning stuff last spring when a bunch of pigeons spent the night on that statue of y'all's ancestor, Mr. James Royce Wooten. Well, you know how pigeons are. They just went to the bathroom *all over* Mr. James Royce. Naturally, Biggie had me scrub the stuff off. That's why that bill goes under *P* for 'pigeon.' Simple, see?" Butch stood up and stretched. "Well, I better run.

Meredith Michelle's watching the store for me, and she can't add worth a flip. Last Friday, she charged Mrs. Oterwald two ninety-eight for a five-foot ficus and six long-stemmed red roses. I declare!"

"Morning, J.R.," Paul and Silas said after Butch had left.

I put two quarters in the Coke machine and pulled out a Big Red. "How do you like police work, so far?"

"I don't know," he said. "Butch seems to have adopted some rather unconventional procedures during his tenure."

"How come you talk funny?"

Paul and Silas smiled. "I am rarely accused of quixotic speech patterns except when I visit you and Cousin Biggie here in Job's Crossing. Perhaps I should modify my speech to fit the vernacular of the people."

I sat down in a chair next to the desk and commenced rubbing neat's-foot oil into the pocket of my glove. Just then, Mr. H. C. Crouch, who owns the newspaper, came in carrying a pad and pencil. He walked over to the desk where Paul and Silas had gone back to his files and said, "I've come to interview you about the murder of our mailman." He took a seat in the chair opposite the desk and crossed his chubby legs. He was wearing black cowboy boots with red half-moons inlaid on the sides. "The people want to know. Have you solved the case yet?"

"Well, er," Paul and Silas said, "we're working on it."

"What have you done so far? Give me some facts, son. I go to press at five."

"Well, you see, sir," Paul and Silas said, "in police matters, sometimes it's better to play things close to the vest. One doesn't want to tip off the killer what we're about."

Mr. Crouch grinned and his chin almost disappeared. "You ain't done a friggin' thing, have you? You don't know who done it and ain't likely to find out because the only reason you got this job was because you happen to be that Weatherford woman's kinfolk. You got any experience in police work?"

"Well . . ."

Mr. Crouch stood up. "Just what I thought," he said. "Well, maybe I'll just write an editorial instead of a news story. We need us a real cop in this town." With that he walked out the door, his boots clicking on the concrete floor.

Paul and Silas sat for the longest time after Mr. Crouch left, just staring out the window with his chin in his hand.

Finally, I spoke up. "Want me to help you solve Luther's murder?"

"Murder? Cousin J.R., where did you get the idea Luther Abernathy was murdered?"

"On account of you said somebody bashed in the back of his head."

"Whoa! I never said another party was involved. I merely posed a question. Surely there's a logical explanation."

"You mean like maybe he bashed his own head in and then climbed back in his car and drove it in the ditch? I didn't see any blood around on the ground where we found him."

Paul and Silas stopped messing with his papers and stared at me. "You're right! How do *you* think it happened?"

"Me? I'm just a little kid. How would I know?" I put my glove and oil back in the sack and started toward the door.

"Wait a minute, Cousin," Paul and Silas said. "Perhaps I should explore the site of the accident. How would you like to ride out there and show me where it happened?"

"OK."

When we came out onto the sidewalk, we saw Meredith Michelle leaving Butch's flower shop wearing a short red bandanna skirt with a white halter top. Paul and Silas's ears turned redder than that skirt.

Meredith Michelle saw us and came over to where we were standing. "Hey, J.R.," she said, tossing her big old hair and looking right at Paul and Silas. "How you doin', Chief Paul and Silas?"

"We're real busy right now," I said.

Paul and Silas blushed tomato soup red. "Morning, Miss Meredith Michelle," he said. "Butch was speaking about you only a few minutes ago."

Meredith Michelle laughed low down in her throat and batted her eyes. "I hope he said something nice."

"He said you couldn't add worth a dern," I said. "Come on, Paul and Silas. We gotta go examine the crime scene."

"Oooh, how exciting," Meredith Michelle said.

"Yes, ma'am," Paul and Silas said. "J.R. was just about to show me where the accident occurred that took the life of Luther Abernathy."

"The crime scene," I said.

"Oh, my gracious," Meredith Michelle said. "Why, I've never been to a *crime scene* before."

Paul and Silas pretty near ran over me getting to the car to open the door for her. Naturally, I had to ride in the backseat.

"Go out past the water tower," I said, then sat back to look out the window on account of Meredith Michelle was talking her old head off.

"Did you know I was crowned Miss Ark-La-Tex last fall?"

"I must say, I'm not at all surprised — a young lady with your charms," Paul and Silas said. "How did it feel to wear the crown?"

Meredith Michelle tilted her head and fiddled with her hair. "It felt . . . wonderful! Ever since I was real little, all I ever wanted in life was to be Miss Ark-La-Tex. Why, I used to spend hours twirling my little baton out on our front porch. That was my talent, twirling. I worked out a twirling routine to a medley of songs from *Phantom of the Opera*. It was very effective. I won the swimsuit *and* the question-and-answer portions of the pageant."

"My, my," Paul and Silas said. "What was the question?"

"They asked me what I'd do to help the developing nations compete in our modern world."

"That sounds like a tough question," Paul and Silas said.

"Not for me it wasn't."

"What did you tell them?" I asked.

"I said, 'What I would do to help the developing nations to compete in our modern world is I would send a team of Mary Kay consultants around to every developing nation to teach the women makeup and skin care because that would raise their self-esteem — and with enough self-esteem, we women can change the world!' You should have heard the audience applauding when I walked off that stage."

"Pull over here," I said. "It's on the left."

Meredith Michelle sat on the fender of the police car while me and Paul and Silas went down into the ditch.

"What stopped the car?" Paul and Silas wanted to know.

I pointed to the ground. "That's what stopped it. The car took a nosedive down into this ditch. The back wheels were dern near sticking up in the air."

Paul and Silas scratched his head. "No way he could have crushed the back of his head. He would have been thrown toward the windshield. Was his face cut up any?"

"Not a scratch," I said. "Just the back."

Paul and Silas commenced walking around looking at the ground and mumbling to himself. "Ground's torn up from the bulldozer. Any signs of struggle would have been obliterated."

"I'm hot!" Meredith Michelle called from the car.

Of *course* Paul and Silas just *had* to do something.

"Just one moment, pretty lady," he said,

scrambling back up the embankment.

He opened the trunk of his car and took out a blanket and a can of soda from a cooler he'd brought along.

"I could handle a Big Red," I said, but nobody heard me. Paul and Silas was leading Meredith Michelle to the shade of a sweet gum tree a few yards from the car. He spread out the blanket for her to sit on and handed her the drink.

I had started over there thinking I might enjoy a little shade, too, when I saw something shiny on the ground. I picked it up and when I did I saw something brown and sticky on my hand. When I looked down, the grass was mashed flat in a path that led straight to the tree where Paul and Silas was spreading the blanket. Brown streaks were mixed up in the mashed-down grass. I touched the brown stuff. It was sticky. I smelled. It was blood.

"Stop!" I yelled. "Don't sit down!"

I yanked the blanket out of Paul and Silas's hands and threw it aside. Sure enough, there was more blood all over the place. Near the tree trunk I saw a big rock. I picked it up and showed it to Paul and Silas.

"Bless my soul," he said, picking something off the rock and holding it up to the light. "What does this look like to you, J.R.?"

"It looks like hairs off Luther Abernathy's head," I said. "Put it in your car for evidence. Let's look some more."

When I got home, Willie Mae was setting a bowl of garlic cheese grits on the table next to a platter piled high with big slabs of chicken-fried steak.

"Go in there and wash up," she said. "Lunch is ready."

"Where's Biggie?" I asked, heading toward the sink.

"Don't wash your nasty hands over my clean dishwater," she said. "Go in the bathroom. Miss Biggie went down to the post office to mail her letter."

I went upstairs to wash my hands and put away my glove. Booger was sitting on top of my rat cage when I got to my room. My rats were looking up at him and shaking like minnows. I picked Booger up and carried him downstairs to the kitchen. Biggie and Rosebud were sitting at the table. The puppy, Bingo, was sitting under Rosebud's chair.

"Now, look at you handlin' that cat," Willie Mae said. "You gonna have to wash your hands all over again."

"Never mind," Biggie said. "A little cat never hurt anybody. Let's eat. I'm hungry enough to eat a boiled jackrabbit." She speared a piece of meat and put it on my plate.

"I'm not hungry," I said.

"Well, now, don't that just beat the goose gobblin'," Rosebud said. "I never in my life seen you when you wouldn't lay a lip around chicken-fried steak."

I told them what we'd found.

"What did you do with the shiny thing?" Rosebud asked.

"I don't remember — wait." I dug down into my pocket. "Here it is!" I held it up for the others to see.

Rosebud took it and turned it over in his hand. "Could be part of a buckle off a mailbag, I reckon. Good work, young'un."

I had to work hard to keep a grin from spreading all over my face while I told her about the rock with hair and blood on it.

"What do you reckon we ought to do about this, Biggie?" I asked.

"I don't know what you're going to do, but I'm going to take myself down to the police station and have a look at that evidence," Biggie said. "Whoever robbed this town of its only mailman deserves to cool his heels in the jailhouse for a good long time. My land, everybody in our zip code must have been down at that post office

111

today. I had to wait ten minutes just for the chance to push my letter down the mail slot." She helped herself to another helping of butter beans. "Yessiree-bob! I'll catch the feller that did in Luther Abernathy or die trying!"

As it turned out, she almost did.

8

At four-thirty that afternoon, me and Rosebud got in Biggie's car and drove to the ballpark, which is at the end of Scroggins Road. Across that road, there used to be a honky-tonk. Folks used to go there and buy unlicensed liquor and dance the dirty bop, but the Baptists had it closed when the town built the Little League park on account of it wasn't a wholesome place for little kids to be playing ball next to. Now they have a youth center, which is mostly used by senior citizens for bingo. The ballpark has wooden bleachers behind home plate and a big chicken-wire fence to protect the fans from getting hit by balls. Over to the left is a tin concession stand and two privies, one for girls and one for boys.

DeWayne was picking wildflowers in right field when we drove up. The rest of the Yankees, our team, were warming up on the field. I won't tell you how practice went because it was a disaster. DeWayne kept picking flowers while Regis Lumpkin, our pitcher, didn't put the ball anywhere close to home plate. I just as well have saved my neat's-foot oil, because my glove never came in contact with a ball. A few parents sat in the stands, and Mr. Hoss Henderson was sitting in his pickup by the road watching practice. Mr. Dick Little, who coaches our arch enemies, the White Sox, was standing behind home plate yelling at his team. Mr. Little is from Ohio and moved to Kemp County to work at Birdsong's poultry business. He quit, though. I heard Mrs. Moody tell Biggie that Mr. Birdsong said if he hadn't quit, he'd have had to fire him anyway — for cruelty to chickens.

"What had he done?" Biggie asked.

"Oh," Mrs. Moody said, "well, egg production fell off sharply while Ben had Dick cleaning out the henhouses. The hens were not sleeping at night, and they were losing their feathers, too. Ben said it took him a long time, but he finally found out what was causing it."

"And what was it?" Biggie asked

"It was that Dick Little. He had taken a boom box in there and had it turned up as high as it would go. It kept playing 'Louie, Louie' over and over again. Well, when Ben confronted him, he said it was his favorite song and he had a right to hear it. Ben told him not if it was costing the company money, and that's when Dick Little went storming out of there making all kinds of threats about how things were about to change around here."

I looked at Mr. Little as he talked to Rosebud. He reminded me of a little bantam rooster with his short legs and his beaky nose and thin lips. He had a bald spot in the back of his head, and now his red hair was blowing in the wind all around it like a rooster's comb. "You guys might as well forfeit now and save us all some trouble," Mr. Little said to Rosebud. "None of them boys can pitch — not hit, either, if you ask me."

Rosebud grinned a slow grin. "Just you be here Saturday night," he said.

Mr. Little sniffed, strutted over to his blue Toyota, and drove off about the same time Mr. Henderson decided to stroll over to talk to Rosebud.

"Your boys ain't looking so good," he said. "I made all-state in high school. Mind if I stick around and help out a little?"

"Reckon not," Rosebud said. "We ain't proud. Boys, hit the field again, and we'll hit a few for Mr. Hoss here."

Well, Mr. Henderson sure knew what he was doing. Before long, he had DeWayne catching grounders, and Regis actually got one or two over the plate. I hit off him every time I came up to bat, though. You'd have to be blind not to. We worked out another hour until the sun went down; then Mr. Henderson promised to come back and help us the next day.

As we walked back to our cars, he hitched up his one overall strap and stuffed a wad of Brown Mule in his mouth. "Can't stand that Little," he said. "He ain't nothing but a cocky little banty rooster." He spit a stream of tobacco juice at a dandelion on the ground. "That ain't all, either. He's been takin' his boys out to the creek and playing army with them since early March."

"How come?" Rosebud asked.

"He's getting um ready to belong to that there 'Empire of Texas' when they get grown."

"What's that?" I asked.

"It's one of them militia clubs. See, they claim the state of Texas ain't part of the U.S. of A., doncha know. Claim when we joined the Union it wasn't legal, so they don't have to obey the laws of Texas *or* the nation."

"Ooowee," Rosebud said.

"*Ooowee*'s right," Mr. Henderson said. "Them idiots claim they can make Texas secede from them other states. They're settin up their own gov'mint with a emperor and ambassadors and all like that."

"I knowed a revolutionary feller once," Rosebud said, throwing bats into the trunk of the car, "old Louie Landry. He wanted to make the whole nation vegetarians on account of him and his people lived downwind of the packing plant in Lake Charles while he was a young'un. He said it affected him right much . . . the smell, doncha know."

"Rosebud!" I said. "We got to be getting on home."

Rosebud whistled under his breath all the way home.

"How come you're so happy?" I asked. "Even with Mr. Henderson to help, we must be the sorriest team that ever was."

"I ain't worried."

"I bet that reminds you of a story."

"Nope," Rosebud said and wouldn't say another word all the way home.

When we got home, we found that Sen. Lefty Lovelace had come for a visit without even waiting for Biggie's letter. He is not much taller than me and wears white suits and carries a cane with a gold parrot's head on top. He's got light blond hair, kind of longish, and a red face. He looks like he might have had a bad case of acne when he was a kid. He has a real-live chauffeur named Gilbert, who is Mexican and does

117

not speak one word of English. Biggie right away moved the senator and Gilbert into the garage apartment out back of our house.

The senator and Biggie were sitting in the parlor drinking iced tea when I came downstairs after washing up. I tried to sneak past the door, but Biggie caught me.

"Come in here, J.R. I want you to meet our guest. This is Sen. Lefty Lovelace. He's come all the way from Austin just to see us."

"Put 'er there, cowboy," the senator said, sticking out his little pink hand. "Come on in here and tell me all about your baseball team."

"We're no good, and Rosebud doesn't care. What's for supper?"

"Willie Mae's making crawfish étouffée," Biggie said, "with Creole corn bread and pecan tarts for dessert."

"Hot tamale!" said the senator, rubbing his little round tummy. "Haven't had any good fresh crawfish since the last time I bellied up to a banquette at Galatois, down in old New Orleans. Biggie, did I ever tell you about the time I almost pled a case in front of the federal court down there? There was this —"

Just then, Willie Mae stuck her head in the door. "Dinner's on," she said.

The table was set in the dining room with

118

Biggie's damask tablecloth and her good china with the Wooten family crest on it. Willie Mae and Rosebud ate in the kitchen with Gilbert. I wanted to eat with them, but Biggie made me sit in the dining room and wear a clean shirt.

After we finished eating, Willie Mae came in and poured coffee out of Biggie's silver pot.

"I smell ribs," I said. "How come . . ."

Willie Mae gave me a look.

"I swan, Biggie," the senator said, unwrapping a big black cigar, "I haven't enjoyed a meal so much since I left Austin. Naturally, we eat right well when the legislature's in session. Them lobbyists, you know, they'll wine you and dine you 'til the world looks level."

"You may not get to keep your job long," I said, just to make conversation. "I heard there's some men that want to take over the state and turn it into an empire."

"Where on earth did you hear that?" Biggie asked.

"From Mr. Hoss Henderson. He says Mr. Dick Little and some of the others want to split Texas away from the rest of the states. Can they do that?"

Biggie set her coffee cup down and wiped her mouth with her napkin. "Of course not.

How silly!" She turned to the senator. "It's still daylight. Why don't we go out and sit on the porch?"

"I could use a little spot of something to relax me," the senator said. "I have a bottle in my bag. Would you join me in a little bourbon and branch, Biggie?"

Rosebud came through the kitchen door. "Miss Biggie, you know Willie Mae don't —"

"Rosebud," Biggie interrupted, "will you prepare a glass of bourbon and water for the senator and a small one for me? No, keep your seat, Lefty. We can provide refreshments for our guests." She stood up. "We'll be on the porch, Rosebud."

I gathered a bunch of pecans and sat on the steps so I could chunk them at squirrels. The senator scooted his chair real close to the porch rail and propped his little bitty feet on the rail. After Rosebud had brought the drinks, the senator pulled a big black cigar out of his pocket and lit it with a gold lighter. He took a deep drag and sent out a cloud of blue smoke.

"Ahhh," he said, "this is real living — good food, good company, good liquor, and a quiet street in a small town. I just might retire here someday, Biggie."

"It's the finest spot on earth," Biggie said. "You couldn't ask for a better place to live.

Don't you agree, J.R.?"

"Huh?" I said, drawing down on a big gray squirrel.

"I said Job's Crossing is a fine place to live."

"Pretty good."

The senator picked up two pecans and cracked them together in his palms. "Just pretty good, son?"

"Well," I said, "seems like all we been doing lately is solving murders. It don't seem to me like most places have so many people killing each other all the time."

"Whoa-ho," the senator said, "the lad's got an imagination."

"I do not!" I said, getting up. "We had our mailman murdered this very week, and before that it was the mayor and the undertaker and, uh, oh yeah, Mr. Firman Birdsong!"

"You don't say," said the senator. "On the surface, it looks so peaceful."

Biggie took a sip of her drink. "Evil lives in the best of places, Lefty. And you can take it to the bank with you that I won't let murder go unpunished in this town."

"How did the mailman die?"

"Someone bashed his head in with a rock," I said.

Biggie gave me a look. "At first, it appeared to be a car wreck," she said, "but J.R. is right. We later discovered that he'd been struck on the back of his head with a blunt instrument — probably a rock."

"Me and Biggie and Rosebud found him," I said. "Then we had to go to Mr. Henderson's house to get him to bring his bulldozer and pull the car out of the ditch. Miz Henderson's got a picture of a dead woman on her mantle."

"I used to know some Hendersons in Wills Point," Senator Lovelace said. "Went to school with a girl — let's see. Sibyl Henderson — we called her Alice the Goon because her arms were so long."

Just then, we heard brakes screeching, then a big crash. The first thing I saw was Buddy Duncan fly through the air, then land in the street beside Biggie's car. His motorcycle flipped over and landed beside him, still running. I could see gas leaking onto the pavement.

In an instant, Rosebud was down the driveway and had switched off the engine. He knelt beside Buddy. Me and Biggie and the senator sat there stunned for a minute, then the three of us got up and started toward them, but before we could get there, Rosebud had Buddy on his feet and was half-carrying him to the house.

"He don't appear to be hurt bad," Rosebud said. "But, Miss Biggie, you'd best take him in and let Willie Mae look him over. I'll get his bike off the road."

We sat Buddy down at the kitchen table while Willie Mae got a basin of soapy water and a clean rag. She mopped the dirt off his face and arms.

"He ain't nothin' but skint up," she said, setting a glass of ice water in front of Buddy. "You hurt anywhere, boy?"

"I'm OK, I think," Buddy said. "But, Miss Biggie, I've gone and put a dent in your car." He put his two hands over his face. "My daddy's gonna kill me for sure!"

"How did it happen?" Biggie asked.

"Near as I can figure, I must have skidded on some acorns on the street." He sighed. "But, to tell the truth, I guess I was going too fast."

Rosebud came in the back door. "Bike's OK. But, Miss Biggie, there's a dent in your fender, and it's right over a tire. Gonna have to get that fixed first thing tomorrow."

"Oh, yes'm," Buddy said. "You take it to my daddy's shop. He'll fix it for you. I'll work every day after school and all day Saturday 'til it's paid for."

"That's a deal," Biggie said, patting him on the shoulder. "Do you want Rosebud to carry you home in the car?"

"No'm," he said. "I can ride — and thank y'all for taking care of me and all." He swallowed the last of his water. "I better be getting on home."

We watched from the front porch as Buddy zoomed off down the street.

"He seems like a real nice boy," Biggie said.

"Luther said he'd been caught stealing hubcaps over in Longview," I said.

Biggie yawned. "Don't believe everything you hear," she said. "Well, I'm off to bed." She turned to the senator, who was leaning back in a porch rocker with his eyes closed. "You need anything, Lefty?"

"Not one thing, Biggie," he said. "I'm worn to a frazzle myself. Soon's I finish this cigar, I'm heading for the old corral."

"Sleep well then," Biggie said. "Breakfast's at eight, and Willie Mae doesn't like to be kept waiting."

9

I woke up in a bad mood the next morning because I'd had a nightmare about baseball. In my dream, all the White Sox had grown to be seven feet tall and were beating the pants off us for the championship. They had tied up DeWayne Boggs and were using him for third base. Rosebud was their batboy, and I was trying to hit the ball using a bass fiddle for a bat. When I opened my eyes and wiggled my left foot, it felt tingly from Booger lying on it all night long. I kicked hard and sent Booger flying. He gave me a dirty look and bounded out the door with his tail in the air.

By the time I had pulled on shorts and T-shirt and come downstairs, Willie Mae was polishing the top of the stove. I didn't see a sign of breakfast anywhere.

"What am I supposed to do, starve?" I asked.

Willie Mae walked to the sink and rinsed out her polishing rag, then hung it over the dish drainer. She didn't say a word, just looked at the clock over the stove. The clock showed 10:30.

I sat down at the table and started playing race cars with the salt and pepper shakers.

"You break Miss Biggie's momma's cut crystal, and you be in trouble," Willie Mae said.

"Well, I'm hungry."

"Whinin' ain't gonna get you nothin'."

I got up and started out the door. "Nobody cares about me," I said.

"Get you a biscuit off the counter and get out of here. Ain't I busy enough with that senator and his flunky here? I got to listen to you, too?"

I reached for a biscuit. "Can I at least have this last piece of cold bacon?"

Willie Mae had turned her back to me and was peeling turnips at the sink. She nodded her head, so I took the bacon and stuffed it in my biscuit, then headed for the front porch. As I passed the living room, I saw Biggie and the senator on the settee. They were jammed up together like two fleas on a frozen dog. Biggie had her big photo album on her lap.

"This is Royce when he was an Eagle Scout," she said. "I know he doesn't look a bit like me. He favored his daddy from the day he was born."

I stepped inside to say good morning, but

they had their heads together over the album and didn't even see me.

"Why, I think he looks a good bit like you, Fiona," the senator said. He turned and looked at her. His yucky old face was not two inches from hers. "Especially those eyes — blue as the West Texas sky."

Biggie blushed. "And this is his high school graduation. He was fourth in his class. There's no telling where that boy could have gone if he hadn't married —"

"A-hem," I said.

Biggie jumped like she'd been stung by a yellow jacket and shoved herself to the far end of the settee. She frowned at me.

"J.R., get out of the living room with that bacon. You'll have grease all over my good things."

I left without saying a word and went looking for Rosebud. At least, I knew *he* was always glad to see me. I found him in the driveway with the senator's driver, Gilbert. They were looking at the senator's white Caddy and jabbering away at each other in Spanish.

I poked Rosebud on the leg. "Hey, Rosebud," I said.

Rosebud mussed my hair with his hand but didn't look at me. He was frowning like he was trying to understand what Gilbert was saying. Gilbert talks real fast.

"Want to pitch a few?" I asked.

Rosebud kept right on looking at Gilbert.

"Want to hear the dream I had? It was real bad, Rosebud. . . ." I stopped because I could tell he hadn't heard one word I'd said.

I went to the garage and got out my bike, thinking I might just go out and question a few suspects. It was a cinch Biggie wasn't thinking about poor Luther's murder. Maybe I'd just solve the thing all by myself. Then they'd notice me for sure.

I rode my bike down to the square and turned right at Handy's House of Hardware. The town was pretty deserted except for a few cars in front of the Owl Café and around the courthouse. I waved at Mr. Thripp, who was sweeping the sidewalk in front of Miss Mattie's tearoom, but he didn't see me.

Just as I was passing Miss Dossie Phelps's antique shop and tanning salon, I happened to glance in and see her dusting the green depression glass in the window. Biggie will never buy any depression glass on account of she says when she was a girl they used to give the stuff away for pitching pennies at the carnival. She said nobody would have depression glass in their houses unless they were too poor to buy a real set of dishes.

Miss Dossie waved at me, so I thought I'd just drop in for a chat.

Today she was wearing a peach-colored dress that floated around her when she walked and some coral earrings that hung almost all the way to her shoulders.

"Hey, J.R.," she said. "You already broke your Biggie's new platter?"

"Uh-uh," I said. "I'm just browsing."

"I got in some new baseball cards. They're over yonder in that pasteboard box on the floor. You want to go through those?"

"I'm not into baseball cards."

"Well, here's something I bet you'll like." She dived down into a box under the counter and came up holding a dirty baseball. "It's signed by Yank Koenig, pitcher for the Center Point Cardinals back in '48. He was the star of the Northeast Texas Baseball League back then."

"They had a league?"

"Sure. Semipro. All the little towns used to have a team." She went back to dusting her dishes. "If you find anything you like, let me know and I'll make you a good price on it."

Mostly the box held old letters and deeds and picture postcards, but from down in the bottom I pulled out a leatherette-covered book. It was an old high school annual from Will's Point dated 1956. I sat down on the floor and commenced thumbing through it. The kids looked real weird. The girls all had on sweaters with little white collars and big, fat skirts. The boys all wore their hair like LeRoy Peoples down at the Eazee Freeze out on the bypass — greased down on the sides with sideburns all the way to the bottoms of their ears. I picked it up and took it over to the counter, where Miss Dossie had started going over some tickets.

"How much for this?"

She picked it up and turned it over. "What do you want with this old thing?"

"I like history. How much?"

Miss Dossie pulled out a rag and dusted the annual off. "I'd have to get a dollar fifty."

I dug down in my pocket and came up with three quarters. "This is all I have."

"Sold."

She pulled a plastic grocery sack out of a drawer and stuffed the book in it. I took it and turned to leave, then thought of something.

"Can I take a look at your tanning bed?" I asked.

"Sure. Tell you what, J.R., you ought to talk to Miss Biggie about taking a few tanning sessions. That woman's white as Wonder Bread."

"Yes'm," I said. I was already heading for the back room.

The bed was still there, looking like a chrome coffin. I ran my hand over the smooth surface; then, looking over my shoulder to see if Miss Dossie had followed me, I turned the switch on the side. The lights came on bright as the sun, I turned it off real fast, then went on into the next room, the one with the painted ladies on the walls. As I was examining the rows of bottles on the shelves, I saw something move at the window. I looked around and who should I see but Buddy Duncan? He was walking real fast and carrying a package. He kept glancing behind him. I decided he looked guiltier than a dog with a chicken in his mouth, so I might just tail him and find out what he was up to. I had plenty of time before Willie Mae got lunch on the table. I ran back to the front of the store, and as I was leaving Miss Dossie called after me, "Don't forget your book!"

"Keep it for me," I said as the door slammed behind me.

I hopped on my bike and pedaled fast as I could around the corner and into the alley behind the store. I hid my bike next to a dumpster behind Itha's House of Hair and, hugging the buildings, inched my way toward the back of the antique shop. Just before I got there, I ducked into a doorway and peeked around to see if Buddy was still there. He was, and you'll never guess what he was doing. He was sitting on Miss Dossie's back stoop with his head in his hands, bawling his eyes out.

I figured he had to quit bawling sometime, so I leaned against the building and waited. I'd never seen a high school kid cry before. His shoulders shook like he was having a chill, and he sobbed digging his fists into his eyes. After a long time, he quit and wiped his face on his sleeve. He stood up real slow like an old man, picked up his package, and started down the alley. He disappeared behind a lean-to where Miss Dossie stores stuff. Just as I was about to start tailing him, I heard his bike roar off down the alley. Naturally, I gave up. There's no way a kid on a bicycle can tail a teenager on a motorcycle, so I decided to go over to Plumley's Rexall to think things over over a strawberry milk shake.

Plumley's is across the square from the courthouse. I go there for a malt or a cherry Coke when I'm out of money on account of Biggie has a charge account there. She doesn't care if I put things on her bill as long as I don't overdo it. I parked my bike out front and took a seat on the stool in front of the pink marble soda fountain and waited for Miss Jewelene MacLeod to come take my order. Pretty soon, she came out of the kitchen wiping her hands on a towel.

"Hey, J.R. The usual?"

I thought for a minute. Normally, I'll have a strawberry milk shake with whipped cream and a cherry on top, but for some reason I wasn't in the mood for that today.

"Uh-uh," I said. "I'll just have a frosted Coke."

I rested my elbows on the cool marble and watched as Miss Jewelene scooped up two dips of vanilla ice cream and put them in a tall frosted glass. Next she held the glass under the fountain and squirted Coke on top. It foamed up and ran over the sides.

"Want a cherry?" she asked, wiping the glass with her towel.

"Two," I said. "You seen Paul and Silas?"

Miss Jewelene looked up at the ceiling, thinking. "I believe he was in here this morning — or was that yesterday? I know he went running out without finishing his coffee when he spotted Butch headed this way." She leaned in so close I could smell her Listerine. "Butch makes him nervous, doncha know."

"How come?"

Miss Jewelene rolled her eyes. "Well, if you don't know . . . it sure isn't my place —"

She didn't get a chance to finish on account of I jumped off the stool and headed out the glass doors, leaving pretty near all my frosted Coke behind. I'd seen Buddy Duncan walking down the sidewalk real fast.

I looked to the left and spotted him turning the corner onto Apple Street. I plastered myself next to a building and watched him pause and look all around before turning into the old compress building across the alley behind Handy's House of Hardware. I knew that was a storehouse where Mr. Handy stored all the junk he couldn't fit into the main store.

By now, it was plain to me that Buddy was up to something. I'd have to investigate further. I tiptoed closer, thinking I'd just have a look, only the door had a frosted glass panel. All I could see was shadows moving around inside. Taking a chance that there might be windows, I went into the alley behind the building. Sure enough, there was one dirty window just above a dented and rusty tin garbage can. If I could just stand on that can without falling over, I could see inside. I climbed on the can and cupped my hands over my face and peered inside. When my eyes got used to the dim light, I saw a room with flaking plaster walls and a gray-brown cement floor. Against one wall I could see a library table with longish wooden boxes piled on top. One of the boxes was open, and a man wearing camouflage fatigues was pulling brand-new rifles out of it. Suddenly he raised one of the rifles and aimed it at a man sitting behind a green metal desk. The man was Mr. Jim Bob Matkin, husband of Mrs. Twyla Matkin, the lady who was trying to get into the Daughters. On the wall behind the desk were some maps and a strange-looking flag. When Mr. Matkin saw the man pointing the gun, he jumped up and started shaking his fist and hollering his head off. I could hear him shouting but couldn't make out the words. Directly here came Buddy, who must have been under the window where I couldn't see him. He put his package on the table, then patted Mr. Matkin on the back and commenced talking to him. In a little while, Mr. Matkin calmed down and took his seat behind his desk.

I rested my chin in my hands and waited to see what was going to happen next. What did happen was a big surprise. The siren on top of the firehouse went off, signaling it was noon. It scared me so bad I jumped and fell off the trash can, which turned over and rolled down the alley, making an awful racket. I heard army boots pounding the floor inside the room. The door flew open and, as I sat on the ground rubbing my knee, a huge shadow fell over me.

10

I found myself staring up into a pair of cold gray eyes mean enough to melt an icicle. They were glaring out of the head of Mr. Jim Bob Matkin. Mr. Matkin was short, but his shoulders and arms near about busted the seams out of the army green shirt he was wearing. His hair, dirty blond and greasy, fell over his forehead. He has a face that's bigger at the bottom than it is on the top, and his wet red lips look like they belong on a chimpanze. When he opened his mouth to speak, his voice sounded more like a grizzly bear than a man.

"What tha' blazes you doin here, boy?" he growled.

I got to my feet, still rubbing my knee, and commenced talking fast. "Who, me?" I said. "I wasn't doing nothing — except chunking rocks at some mangy old tomcat. You see, sir, that cat's been bothering everybody around here, tumping over their trash cans and stuff, so I told Miss Jewelene over at Plumley's, I said I'd see if I couldn't scare him off. Well, sir, he runs down this alley, and I'm hot on his tracks with a pocket full of rocks when durned if he don't slam-dunk himself smack into that garbage can right there —"

Mr. Matkin held up his hand. "Shut your gopher trap, boy." He bent down, picked me up by my elbows, and held me where I had to stare into those evil eyes of his. "Now hear this," he said real slow. "If I ever find you playin' around here again, I'll whup your ass 'til your hat flies off. Do you read me, boy?"

I nodded.

"Speak up!" His lips slapped together and I felt a spray of spit hit my face.

"Yes, sir!"

"Then git on outta here."

I got.

"Biggie!" I yelled, bursting in the front door.

Biggie and the senator were sitting at the dining table when I skidded around the corner. They had napkins on their laps and were just starting to eat.

"J.R., how many times am I going to have to speak to you about slamming that door? Oh, my sakes, look at you. If you aren't a mess. What in the world's happened?"

I sat down and proceeded to give her a full

report of my investigation.

"You know what I think, Biggie? I betcha those men are some of those *Empire of Texas* guys. You reckon?"

"I expect so," Biggie said, taking my chin in her hands. "It doesn't matter. What I'm concerned about is you putting yourself in danger. If I ever find out you've been spying on people again . . ." She pulled me close and threw her arms around me. "You could have been hurt." She kissed the top of my head. "Promise me you won't do that again."

I looked over Biggie's shoulder at a platter of fried chicken. The steam floating out of the gravy boat crawled into my nostrils and made my mouth water. Fresh field peas and yellow corn bread were mixed up together on the senator's plate, and he was raking them into his mouth with his knife. All of a sudden, I was hungry enough to eat the horns off a billy goat.

"OK, I promise." I wiggled out of her grasp. "Can I eat in the kitchen?"

She nodded and, as I left the room, I heard the senator say, "Don't discount the militia groups, Fiona. They have the potential to pose a real threat to the good folks of Texas."

After lunch, I went to my room and lay across my bed. I needed to think about what had happened to me. What were those men planning to do with all those guns? All of a sudden, our little town didn't feel so safe anymore — and I thought this might be a situation that was too big even for Biggie to handle.

I must have fallen asleep, because it was after three when I came back downstairs. Biggie was hanging up the phone.

"Oh, J.R.," she said. "That was the county judge, Judge Hoover. He's just given permission for Hoss Henderson to do the dirt work on the Daughters' Wooten Creek property for a nominal fee."

"Can I have some pie?" I asked.

Biggie rubbed her hands together and started for the stairs. "Go in the kitchen and get you a piece; then tell Rosebud I want him to drive me out to Hoss Henderson's place. Tell him I'll be in my room getting ready."

"Is the senator going?" I asked.

"No. He's gone downtown to look around," Biggie answered from top of the stairs.

"Then I'll go with you!" I yelled. But I don't think she heard me, on account of by then water was already running in the bathroom.

The sky had turned black in the west when we pulled into the Hendersons' driveway. The air was cool and the wind was kicking up little dust devils in the yard. Biggie's skirts whipped around and slapped her legs when she got out of the car. She turned back toward Rosebud, who was in the driver's seat. "Honk the horn so they'll know we're here."

Rosebud gave two short beeps, and pretty soon Mrs. Henderson appeared on the front porch. The wind blew her hair loose from the bun she always wore it in, and it fell around her face in little ringlets. She looked almost pretty — for an old woman. The dogs came walking on their bellies out from under the house. This time, they didn't bark, just wagged their tails as they wrapped themselves around Mrs. Henderson's legs.

"Go on, dogs," she said, waving her apron at them. "Afternoon, Miss Biggie. Hidy, J.R., Rosebud."

"Is Hoss around?" Biggie asked. "I need to talk a little business with him."

"He's over grading Judge Hoover's driveway," Mrs. Henderson said. "Y'all come on in. He'll be back directly."

"We might just drive over there," Biggie said. "Doesn't the judge live over on Ferndale Road?"

"Yes'm, that's right. You just turn left about three-quarters of a mile up thataway."

She pointed to the left. "He lives in that green house with the yellow trim."

"I need a drink of water," I said.

Mrs. Henderson smiled a dimply smile. "Come on in the house and I'll get you one."

I looked at Biggie, who nodded.

"Stay in there," Mrs. Henderson said, pointing to the room where Mr. Henderson's recliner sat right opposite the television. "I'll bring it to you. I don't want nobody to see my messy kitchen."

I walked over to the mantelpiece to have another look at Mrs. Henderson's momma in her casket. I was looking at Mr. Henderson's sister in her basketball uniform when Mrs. Henderson came back with my water. "She sure is tall," I said.

"Here's you water," she said. "I put it in a paper cup so's you could carry it with you. Scat, now! Your Biggie's waiting."

"Does she ever come to visit?" I asked, still looking at Mr. Henderson's sister. "I sure would like to get a look at ... er ... meet her."

"She's dead," she said, turning back toward the kitchen. "Run along now."

I hollered, "Thanks for the water!" and headed for the car.

We met Mr. Henderson bumping along home on his road grader. He had his hat pulled low on his head on account of the wind had picked up a good bit. You could smell the rain in the air, and off in the distance yellow lightning streaked the sky.

Rosebud stopped the car and waved for Mr. Henderson to pull over so we could talk to him. When he did, he swung himself to the ground and ambled over to the car.

"Hidy do, Miss Biggie."

"Hello, Hoss," Biggie said. "I've got a job of work for you to do for a mighty good cause."

I wasn't very interested in what they were saying, so I wandered through the tall grass by the ditch to see what I could see. I found a brown box turtle hiding under some sycamore leaves. By the time I'd caught him and brought him back to the car, Biggie and Mr. Henderson had finished talking business and were chatting about other things.

"No'm," Mr. Henderson was saying. "Me and my wife are not from around here. We both grew up over in Rains County."

"You don't say?" Biggie said. "Do you happen to know State Senator Lefty Lovelace from Will's Point?"

"Not nobody named Lefty," he said. "Still and all, they was some Lovelaces around there — I recollect one little old runtified feller went to school with us. . . ." Mr.

143

Henderson looked up at the sky. "Gawdamighty, it's fixing to pour down. Excuse me, Miss Biggie. I got to get this here county equipment in the shed."

Biggie waved good-bye as Mr. Henderson turned on the machine and it rumbled to a start. I got in the backseat and put my turtle on the floorboard just as Rosebud was starting up the car.

By the time we got back to town, rain mixed with hail was pelting the car. We dashed into the house just in time to see Willie Mae pulling a pan of tea cakes out of the oven.

"Git over here and sprinkle sugar on these cookies while they hot," she said to me.

I got a spoon out of the drawer and commenced spooning sugar out of the sugar bowl on top of the cookies.

"Not so much," Willie Mae said, waving her spatula at me. "Miss Biggie, I got some fresh coffee here."

Biggie poured herself a mug and flopped down at the table, reaching for a cookie. She took a bite and grinned from ear to ear. "Heaven. There's nothing like being safe in your own home when a storm's brewing outside."

Willie Mae looked hard at Biggie. "Might be there's more than one kind of storm brewing in this town right now."

Biggie wasn't going to let her good mood be spoiled. "Nothing I can't handle," she said, reaching for a third cookie.

Rosebud turned from the stove, where he was pouring himself a cup of coffee. "Where's the senator?"

"Done walked to town. I reckon he's stuck in some store somewhere 'til this rain let up."

"Want me to go get him?" Rosebud asked.

"Drink your coffee first," Biggie said. "He's got sense enough to come in out of the rain."

Willie Mae rolled her eyes like she was not so sure.

"How come Gilbert doesn't go get him?" I asked.

"On account of the senator gave Gilbert the use of his car to go visit some kinfolks he's got down in Mount Enterprise," Willie Mae said. "He left this afternoon."

"I'm going with you," I said to Rosebud. "I left something downtown."

"You ain't goin' nowhere," Willie Mae said. "I need you to shuck these roasting ears for supper."

"Willie Mae! I got to go. It's important."

"Never mind," Rosebud said. "I'll help you and then we'll go."

"I'll help, too," Biggie said. "I like to shuck corn."

Willie Mae spread a newspaper on the table and dumped out enough roasting ears to feed the whole town. "We ain't eating all this for supper," she said when she saw the look on my face. "I'm putting what we don't eat in the freezer."

By the time we got finished with the corn, the rain had slowed down to a drizzle and the sky was turning yellow on the horizon. The air felt cool and the grass and trees looked greener than they had before.

We parked by the square.

"I'll tell you what," I said. "You take half the square and I'll take the other. That'll save time."

"Maybe," Rosebud said, "but first we check the Owl Café and Plumley's. He might of gone somewhere for a little nourishment while it was raining."

"No, he didn't," I said, pointing. "There he is in the antique shop. Come on, Rosebud. I gotta pick up a package I left in there."

I headed for the shop. In the window we could see the senator lean across the counter and say something to Miss Dossie. She was laughing like a double-jawed hyena. Suddenly the senator leaned over and kissed

Miss Dossie right on the mouth. I looked at Rosebud to see if he was watching. He had a look on his face that said he'd seen it all. He opened the door to the shop so hard Miss Dossie's little bell over the door fell on the floor and rolled under a table piled high with old-timey sheet music.

11

The senator looked like he'd swallowed a frog. Miss Dossie just smiled and bent down to pick up her little bell. She slipped it into the pocket of her skirt. "Why, Rosebud and J.R. What are y'all doin' out in this rain? Come on in here and dry off. J.R., where in the world is your raincoat? What's Miss Biggie thinking, letting you come out in this weather?"

"It's not hardly raining anymore," I said. "I guess y'all didn't notice."

Miss Dossie glanced outside at the yellow sky. "Well, what do you know. It must have just this very minute stopped."

"No'm. See, the sidewalks are starting to dry already."

The senator had gotten real interested in a spot on the sleeve of his white suit. He was picking at it with his fingernail. I guess he didn't know he had lipstick smeared all over his face. He nearly jumped out of his skin when Rosebud walked up to him.

"Miss Biggie sent us to fetch you," was all Rosebud said before he headed for the door all stiff-necked. I grabbed my sack off the counter and followed him out. The senator was right behind me.

Nobody was talking in the car going home, so to make conversation, I said, "Mrs. Muckleroy says Miss Dossie's common on account of the way she dresses and all, but I don't believe that. I think she's just a real nice person. Don't you, Senator?"

What I was trying to do was draw him out. I knew he hadn't any business kissing Miss Dossie like that, and he knew it, too. Not after he'd been trying to flirt with Biggie ever since he got to town. I planned to tell Biggie the very first chance I got, and if I could get him to talk about it I'd have even more to tell her.

It didn't work.

The senator just sat there, not even answering me. His neck got red, though.

When we got back to the house, Rosebud parked the car in the garage and, without a word, went into his little house and closed the door behind him. The senator mumbled something about a shower and headed up the stairs to the garage apartment.

I found Willie Mae in the kitchen basting a roast. Biggie was on the phone to Miss Julia talking about the Daughters' project out on the lake. I poured myself a glass of

Snapple from the bottle in the fridge and sat at the kitchen table to watch Willie Mae. The roast had made the whole kitchen smell all garlicky. Willie Mae dumped a bowlful of peeled potatoes into the roasting pan and shoved it back in the oven.

"Yum," I said. "What else are we having?"

"Broccoli —"

"Yuck!"

"— with cheese sauce."

"Yum. What else?"

She glared at me. "You writin' a book?"

"Yes'm," I said. "A cookbook. And I'm putting all your good recipes in it."

That softened her up a little. "Corn on the cob and some of that Jell-O salad you like so much. There's bread pudding for dessert."

Just then, Biggie walked into the kitchen.

"Biggie," I said, "I've got something to tell you."

Biggie was putting on her earrings and looking around for her purse. "Not now, J.R. We're having a called meeting of the executive committee down at the newspaper office. Julia thinks she has the solution to our problems with the land project."

Before I could say another word, Biggie was out the door calling for Rosebud. I wondered if he'd say anything to her about the senator and Miss Dossie.

I went up to my room and lay across my bed, thinking about what we'd seen. The more I thought about it, the madder I got. It was pretty plain to me that Biggie had the candy legs for Senator Lovelace, and up until today I'd thought he felt the same. But the way it looked now, he was just plain two-timing Biggie. I sat on the edge of the bed, picked up my glove, and commenced rubbing it with neat's-foot oil. Then I had a scary thought. Suppose Biggie liked him a lot, even loved him. Suppose she wanted to *marry* him. I made a face. If there was one thing I knew for sure, it was that I didn't want that old baby kisser thinking he could move in here and join our family. I hated the way he was always whispering secrets in Biggie's ear just like they were the only two people in the room. When he wasn't doing that, he was bragging about what a big shot he was in Austin. I was pretty sure Rosebud didn't think so much of him, either. I'd just have to talk to Rosebud about it. He always knew what to do. But I still intended to tell Biggie all about it just as soon as I could get her alone. I sat up and looked out the window. Through the branches of the crepe myrtle tree I could see the sun sinking down behind a bank of black clouds, and I saw a flash of lightning in the distance. Sure as anything, we were in for another frog strangler.

I decided to play with my rats until suppertime. I had rescued Slasher, Crusher, Flash, and Bruiser from Mrs. Moody's garage when they were babies. That was on account of Booger had eaten their mother. I keep them in a cage in my room. They're good pets, even if they are rats. Once, they even helped Biggie solve a murder. As soon as I opened the cage door, Slasher ran up my arm and sat on my shoulder. The others ran around the room sniffing the floor for crumbs. I sprinkled some hamster pellets on the floor and watched them eat until I heard Biggie coming up the stairs.

"Don't open my door!" I yelled. I grabbed my rats and stuffed them in their cage. I went and stood at Biggie's bedroom door.

"Biggie, you're not going to believe this. When me and Rosebud —"

Just then, Willie Mae's voice came from the bottom of the stairs: "Dinner!"

"I could eat a camel," Biggie said, heading out the door.

When we got to the dining room, Senator Lovelace was already seated at the table. He had changed into a pair of blue slacks and a short-sleeved white shirt. His hair was still damp from the shower. He jumped up from his chair when Biggie came in and pulled out a chair for her. "Have a seat, lovely lady," he said, not looking at me. "You look prettier than a pie supper tonight."

Biggie turned pink.

"Pass the meat," I said in a loud voice.

After supper, during which Biggie and the senator ignored me and talked to each other in low voices, we all went into the parlor. I figured I might as well look at the book I'd bought at Miss Dossie's shop, since it was a cinch nobody was going to be talking to me. I was lying on the rug, thumbing through the old pictures, when the senator walked by carrying his third glass of bourbon and branch water. He stumbled over my feet and sloshed a little of his whiskey on my book.

"Oops! Sorry, son," he said, whipping his handkerchief out of his pocket. "Let me get that." As he stooped down to mop up the spill, his hand stopped in midwipe. "Well, if that don't beat old Billy Whiskers," he said, forgetting the highbrow talk he'd learned in Austin.

"Huh?"

Before I knew it, he had flopped down on the floor beside me, carefully blotting up the last of the wet on the page. He flipped the book over to look at the cover.

"Do you know what this is, son?" he

asked. "This is my old high school annual. Yessiree. Wills Point High. Nineteen fifty-six. My senior year. Where'd you get this?"

"Down at Miss Dos— the antique store."

He was turning the pages with a funny little grin on his face. "My, oh, my. If this don't take me back. There's Mrs. Tarpley, the English teacher, and Miss Boon. She taught the girls PE. I had such a crush on her."

By this time, Biggie had come and joined us on the floor. "Show us your picture," she said.

The senator sat cross-legged on the floor and put the book on his lap. "Here," he said. "That's my senior picture." He pointed to a pimply-faced kid with a burr haircut. He was skinny as a rail and wore big, thick glasses.

Biggie didn't seem to notice that. "My land," she said. "You were certainly active."

Sure enough, under his name was a long list of activities he'd been involved in: Band, Debate, National Honor Society, Spanish Club. Nerdy things, like that.

"Didn't you play any sports?" I asked.

The senator colored. "Not too much, son. Ran a little track. Never had much interest in it. 'Let the others be the athletes,' is what my mama always said. 'Frankie Lee,' she used to say, 'you ain't no bigger than a bar of soap after a day's washing. You'd best use the brains God gave you, or you'll never amount to nothin'.' I've always valued that advice, and it's served me well in life." He smiled like he was real pleased with himself and patted his belly.

I took the book and flipped through the pages. It fell open at the girls' basketball team. There, sitting on the gym floor with a towel over his shoulder and two basketballs between his knees, was the senator. "You were water boy for a *girls'* team?" I said.

"I only did that job so I could be close to Miss Boon," he said, trying to take the book from me.

I held on. "Hey," I said. "I see Mr. Henderson's sister. Looky here, Biggie. I saw her picture on the mantle at their house. Boy, she's taller than anybody. Wow!"

Biggie looked at the picture and nodded. "She's tall all right. Looks a good bit like Hoss. Don't you think?"

I nodded. "Mrs. Henderson told me they were twins."

Biggie looked again. "Wonder whatever happened to her."

Biggie's always been curious like that.

The senator was frowning. "I don't remember the Goon having a twin. . . ."

"Huh?" I said.

Just then, there was a loud crash of thunder and the lights went out. We all sat still in the dark for a minute.

"My soul," Biggie said; then she got up and felt her way over to the mantle. "Bring your matches over here, Lefty."

The senator struck a match and lit the candles in the brass candlesticks Biggie always keeps on the mantle. A dim glow filled the room. Biggie sank down on the couch and looked out the window at the rain blowing in on the front porch. Just then, a flash of lightning filled the room. I jumped as another clap of thunder rattled the rafters. Rosebud came bounding in.

"Miss Biggie, the storm's caused a short in the wiring. I smell smoke in the kitchen. Call the fire truck. Quick!"

Biggie picked up the phone, then put it back down. "Dead," she said.

Rosebud was already heading toward the door. "I'll go get um," he said. "Y'all better get outta here. Go up to the garage apartment."

By the time we got to the back door, little fingers of flame were coming out of the wall plug next to the kitchen sink. Biggie pushed me and the senator out the back door, and we ran through the pouring rain to the stairs leading up to the garage apartment.

We watched through the windows as Job's Crossing's only fire truck came whining up our driveway with its lights flashing. Norman Thripp was driving the truck. He had on a big yellow fireman's hat and a yellow slicker. I saw Mr. Handy take the end of the hose and attach it to the fire hydrant next to the street; then, with Rosebud's help, two of the men grabbed the big hose and disappeared through our back door. Mr. Thripp followed, carrying a hatchet.

They hadn't been in the house long before Willie Mae came out of her little house wearing her raincoat. She followed the men into the kitchen, and before long they all came trooping out followed by Willie Mae, who had a scowl on her face that would clabber milk. The men got into the fire truck and drove away. Willie Mae and Rosebud went into their house and closed the door.

12

The next morning, when I came down for breakfast, I found Willie Mae muttering to herself while she mopped the kitchen floor. Biggie had a pail of soapy water and a sponge and was wiping down the cabinets. She wasn't doing a very good job. Biggie's good at a lot of things, but housework's not one of them. Rosebud was standing on a ladder washing the walls and ceiling. Black soot was all over everything, and the smell of smoke was awful. A big hole had been hacked away where the wall switch used to be.

"What's for breakfast?" I asked.

The way they all looked at me, I decided I'd best go outside.

"Where you heading?" Willie Mae said. "Get you a rag out of the sink and start cleaning off that cookstove. When you're through with that, you can start on the icebox."

I got a rag and started swiping at the side of the range. The rag only made black streaks on the white porcelain. I rinsed the rag off in the sink and squeezed the water out. "This is hard work," I said. "Hey, I've got an idea. Since it's already wet in here, why not bring in the garden hose and just wash everything down?"

"You ain't got no more sense than them firemens," Willie Mae said. "Get you some more soap on that rag."

"Where's the senator?" I asked.

"He's gone down to the Owl for his breakfast," Biggie said. "He didn't want to be in the way."

Rosebud mumbled something under his breath.

It was near noon when we finished cleaning the kitchen. Willie Mae took some cold chicken out of the refrigerator and started slicing pieces of breast meat. "Get a loaf of my buttermilk bread out of the freezer," she said to Biggie, "and I'll slice some for sandwiches."

Willie Mae pulled a jar of peach pickles out of the fridge and poured glasses of milk for everybody. I ate three sandwiches and drank two glasses of cold milk.

"I wonder what's happened to Lefty," Biggie said, patting her lips with her napkin.

"Oh, by the way, Biggie, I've been meaning to tell you something."

She stood up. "Later," she said. "I've got to go to town and talk to H. C. Crouch about giving the Daughters some free publicity for our creek project. We've decided to have a rummage sale to help pay for the improvements on the property."

"You'd best see about getting your own property improved first," Willie Mae said. "This kitchen's gonna have to have a new coat of paint."

Biggie looked around the room. Soot was still streaked on every surface, and the ceiling was gray with the stuff. "You're right. I'll see if I can get Floyd and Boyd Vanderslice to come out and give us an estimate."

Rosebud had been standing at the sink eating a peach. He turned and looked at Biggie. "No'm," he said. "We don't need them Vanderslices around here. I'll just go down to Handy's and get the paint and do the job myself."

"Fine," Biggie said. "The job's in your hands, then. I'll be on my way to the newspaper office. Coming, J.R.?"

"Yes'm," I said.

Biggie talked about the Daughters all the way downtown, so I still didn't get a chance to rat on the senator. When we got to the newspaper office, we found the editor, Mr. Crouch, sitting at his big rolltop desk with his feet propped up. Mr. Crouch has skin the color of Silly Putty and lots of silver hair that stands up high on his head. He has little bitty blue eyes and lips like a woman. I once heard Miss Julia say he was going to get sued for harassment one of these days on account of he can't keep his hands off the girls that work the front office. His desk was piled high with back copies of the paper, and sitting right on top of the tallest pile was a picture of a black-haired woman with a face that would sour milk. I couldn't tell whether the expression on her face was a smile or she smelled something really bad.

He put down the magazine he was reading when we came in the room. "Well, if it's not Biggie Weatherford. And is this J.R.? My, oh, my, how they grow. Last time I saw you, you wasn't any bigger than a baby gnat."

"I'm almost thirteen," I said. "Anyway, you just saw me the other day at the police station."

"Was that you?" he said. "Well, slap me baldheaded." He leaned forward and moved a stack of papers off a chair next to his desk. "Have a seat, Biggie. What can I help you with?"

"I heard you got married," Biggie said, once she was settled.

Mr. Crouch leaned forward and plucked

161

the picture off his desk. "Right-o," he said. "Here's my little Filipino baby. She ain't much on looks, but she's hell for stout. That woman can outwork fifteen American gals. And humble? Unlike my last two wives, that old gal don't know the meaning of the phrase *high horse.* I tell you, Biggie, I done got me a winner." He laughed and slapped his knees. He leaned toward Biggie. "And you know what they say: it all looks the same in the dark."

Biggie's lips had gotten thin, but she forced herself to smile. "Yes, well, congratulations. Now, H.C., I suppose you've heard the Lions Club has offered to deed the Daughters a tract of land out on the lake —"

"Mighty right I heard. Julia Lockhart can't talk about anything else. Says you're planning to put a campgrounds out there for the ladies. That right?"

Biggie nodded. "We plan to use it for retreat purposes, but that's not all. We want to make the property available for the community to use. We'll put in picnic tables, barbecue pits, even a little pavilion in case it rains."

Mr. Crouch made a little tent with his fingers and leaned his chin on it. "Umm," he said, his eyes half-closed.

"The thing is," Biggie went on, "we're

going to have to have several fund-raisers to earn the money to put it together. That's where you come in."

Mr. Crouch brightened. "I see, publicity. Naturally, you want to publicize the thing. Well, Biggie, you've come to the right place." He reached into one of the cubby-holes in his desk and brought out a brochure. He spread it in front of Biggie and leaned forward. "Now, here's our deluxe plan. For fifteen hundred, we'll run a half-page ad the first week, two quarter-pages the next two issues, and, as an added bonus, I'll write up a front-page news story about the project."

"Well, I —"

"Too rich for your blood? OK, how about our Plan A? For eight hundred, you get two quarter-pages and a mention in my 'Up and down Main Street' column."

Biggie had been looking out the window at Butch, who was walking down the side-walk with Nathan Lane under his arm. "Wonder why he's carrying that cat around?" she said.

Nathan Lane is Butch's cat, who lives at the florist shop.

"You drive a hard bargain, Biggie," Mr. Crouch said. "Suppose I give you five classifieds and coverage of your grand opening. Two hundred dollars. That's my rock-bottom price."

"You'll cover the opening anyway. It's going to be big news. H.C., honey, what I want you to do is give us some free publicity. Seeing as how you're starting your third term as president of the Rotary Club, it's the least you can do."

"I don't see what that's got to do with it — where is this property, anyway?"

"It's a little triangle of land between Wooten Creek and the west bank of the lake. Used to be used as a dump. Two years ago, the Lions bought it to put up a deer blind. Well, you know most of those old fellows in the Lion's Club are getting up in years. I don't know when I've seen any of them wearing those little red vests and peddling lightbulbs lately. Just as well, I guess. The things didn't last a week. Anyway, they got the blind up, and last year at deer season quite a few of them went out and used it. The only thing was, sitting out in the damp woods in November made their arthritis act up. A few caught colds and of course you remember old man McGuffey died of pneumonia that winter. Their wives made them take the thing down and organize a square-dancing club, which they did, and now they dance at the VFW every other Thursday night."

Mr. Crouch leaned forward in his chair like he had suddenly gotten real interested in what Biggie had to say. Biggie, thinking she had him convinced, went on. "It's a very worthwhile project, H.C., and will be a boon to the county. I know you'll be able to see your way clear to give us some free coverage, being the fine public-spirited citizen that you are."

"Is that the property that used to belong to Fresh as a Daisy? The one they used to dump poultry waste on?"

"That's it," Biggie said. "But Ben Birdsong sold it to the Lions soon after Firman died."

"Y'all don't want that land, Miss Biggie. It's not fit for anything but a dump ground."

Biggie smiled. "Honey, don't you worry about that. We've got a plan. You just give us a little help and we'll —"

"No!" Mr. Crouch stood up. "I'm telling you, you ladies don't need to be running around out there. I'll tell you what. I know a feller that'll most likely take it off your hands for a nice little piece of change. Just let me give him a call, and I'll get back to you." He looked at his watch. "Gawdamighty, look at the time. I'm supposed to be over at the courthouse this very minute." With that, he slammed his hat on his head and was out the door before you could say boo to a goose.

"Well, I'll be switched," Biggie said.

I looked out the window just in time to see Mr. Crouch heading down the street toward the alley behind Plumley's Rexall, the opposite direction from the courthouse.

13

Guess what. Somebody has built a roller-skating rink out by the lake, and Rosebud took me and the team out there last night on account of we did so good at practice. Roller-skating at a rink sure isn't like skating on the sidewalk. That floor is slick! I fell down six times, and once we had a big pileup. Wouldn't you know it, Paul and Silas was out there skating with Meredith Michelle, who was wearing a short skirt with sparkly things on it — like she thought she was in the Olympics or something. The two of them were skating double and staring into each other's eyes so much they didn't even see me on the floor where I'd fallen and was trying to get back up on my skates. They skated right over me and just looked back and laughed. I could have been killed. I really hate girls and am never going to get married. One thing surprised me quite a bit. DeWayne Boggs, who can't walk and chew gum, was all over the place, darting in and out between the other skaters like a cannonball. He said his Aunt Vida used to take him to the rink over in Center Point all the time. He was almost better than Rosebud, who can skate backward and everything.

I was at the concession stand getting a Big Red when Biggie walked in.

"I'm on my way out to see Twyla Matkin," she said, "and thought I'd just stop by for a minute to watch you skate."

"I might be through."

"Through? Why?"

"Well, uh, my feet hurt, that's why. These old skates are too big. I think they're rubbing a blister, Biggie."

"My soul, look at that DeWayne. He's a regular Dick Button. And look; there's Paul and Silas."

"Biggie, I think I'll go with you."

"Is that Meredith Michelle? Why, it sure is. What in the world is she wearing? Oh, well. What did you say, J.R.?"

"I said I think I'll go with you."

"What? To Twyla's? Oh, well, OK, but I don't see why you want to. . . ."

I was already taking off my skates. "Because, uh, I want to see that big bass boat her husband's got. I ain't never seen it up close."

"Haven't ever," Biggie said. "Well, go tell Rosebud you're leaving, then."

The Matkins live in a log house that sits in a grove of trees down a winding road off the highway. It's the neatest house I've ever seen. They have a real Indian totem pole in their front yard. We walked up on the wide front porch, and Biggie knocked with a brass knocker shaped like a widemouthed bass. In a minute Mrs. Matkin came twittering to the door. When we walked in the big front door, my mouth flew open. Stuffed fish and animal heads covered every wall. There was even a whole black bear standing on his hind legs in the entry hall. His teeth were as big as my fingers, and his claws looked like they could take a man's arm off. Mr. Matkin had put a cowboy hat on the bear's head, and a coat was slung over one paw. Over the big stone fireplace Mr. Matkin had hung a big shaggy buffalo head. Fish and birds were everywhere, and for a coatrack he had mounted deer hooves in a row by the front door. A zebra rug was spread on the floor in front of the hearth.

"Wow," I said.

Biggie had an expression on her face I couldn't understand. It reminded me of the way she'd looked when we found Luther — sort of sick and sad at the same time.

"Well, Miss Biggie," Mrs. Matkin said. "My sakes. What a nice surprise."

Mrs. Matkin took Biggie back to the kitchen to make a pot of tea while I stayed behind to look at all the dead animals. I was feeling the fur on a bobcat crouched on the bar when I heard voices in the next room. I jerked my hand away from the cat and tiptoed to the door to see who was talking. Rosebud says one of these days my ears are going to grow big as dinner plates on account of I'm so nosy.

The door was closed except for a tiny crack. If I closed one eye and squinted with the other, I could see a thin slice of the room. It looked like an office of some kind. Mr. Matkin was sitting at a desk. I could only see his elbow and part of his shoulder, but it was him all right. I'd never forget that voice as long as I lived. He was talking on the phone.

"Hang on a minute. Somebody just came in."

I scooted away from the door and hid behind the big black bear. Mr. Matkin came into the room and shouted for his wife.

"Twyla! Get in here!"

Mrs. Matkin came bustling into the room holding a teapot in her hand. "What is it, sweetest?"

"Who's here?" he barked.

"It's nobody but Miss Biggie," she said. "She's come to talk to me about joining the Daughters of the Republic of Texas. Isn't that nice?"

"Humph. I guess it can't hurt anything as long as it doesn't take you away from your main job, which is taking care of your home and husband. In fact, it might just be real helpful if you'd join up with them old bags." Suddenly he grinned, showing big yellow teeth. "Hell, someday you just might be the friggin' First Lady of Texas."

He went back into his office and closed the door, tight this time. I put my ear to the door, though, and heard everything he said.

"It wasn't nobody but that Weatherford heifer — wanting to talk the wife into joining her little old lady society. I told her she could as long as she kept her nose clean. . . . What? . . . No, you don't have to worry about my woman. She knows she better keep her trap shut, or I'll shut it for her. Anyway, it could be helpful to have her in the enemy camp, so to speak. . . . I know what you mean. No, they ain't exactly enemies. That is, unless they decide to go ahead with that damn fool scheme of turning our headquarters into a friggin' ladies' picnic park! Then we'll have to educate um." He laughed a mean laugh. "Yeah, you're right. That might be kind of enjoyable, but, pardner, you don't want to forget our real mission. These old ladies wouldn't make a wart on an elephant's ass compared to that. . . . OK, call me back when you find out more."

I heard the receiver slam down and hurried into the kitchen before he could come out and catch me.

I sat down at the table beside Biggie and commenced swinging my feet. I guess I must have kicked the table leg a couple of times.

"J.R., stop that," Biggie said.

"Biggie, we got to go," I said.

"Why?" Biggie had papers spread out all over the table. "We're conducting business here."

"Because, uh, because I've got ball practice. I can't be late, Biggie."

"J.R., ball practice is not until seven. It's only four. What's the matter with you?"

"I don't feel so well."

Biggie reached over and felt my forehead. "Cool as a cucumber," she said. "Go out and sit on the swing out back."

"Poor baby," Mrs. Matkin said. "How about if I fix you a Dr Pepper? My mama used to always give us Dr Pepper when we felt sick. Are you sick at your stomach?"

"No'm, I've got a headache." I scrunched up my eyes and rubbed my head. "A Big Red might help."

"I don't think I have —"

"J.R., get outside and sit on that swing!"

172

I got. You don't mess with Biggie when she uses that tone. I knew she'd be sorry, though, when I told her what I'd found out, and I was right.

I saved up my news until after ball practice, when Biggie and the senator were sitting on the front porch drinking bourbon and branch water and talking about the governor, who the senator knows personally, and his wife, too.

I waited until the senator was right in the middle of a story about how he'd been at the governor's mansion one time when everybody there was drunker than skunks and the state comptroller rode his motorcycle into the pool and sank like a rock to the bottom.

"Did he drown?" I asked.

"No, but he would have if one of the waiters hadn't been a lifeguard. He dived in, and when he got to the bottom the feller was still sitting on the motorcycle like he didn't even know he was underwater."

I got up off the steps and sat on the porch rail facing Biggie and the senator. "I've got a story," I said, "and it's true."

"Let 'er rip!" the senator said.

"Biggie, Mr. Matkin and the Empire of Texas guys have their headquarters on that land that y'all are getting, and they're going to stop you from doing anything out there."

Of course, Biggie had to know how I knew about it and, of course, I had to tell her all about how I was listening at the office door and heard Mr. Matkin on the telephone. Then I had to remind her about what I'd seen out behind Plumley's because she'd forgotten all about that, what with all the other stuff she'd had on her mind lately.

Biggie reached over and patted my knee. "What a good little detective you are," she said. "You may have saved the Daughters a peck of trouble."

"What are you going to do, Biggie? Forget about the land?"

"Forget it?" Biggie's eyes got wide. "Never! It'll be a cold day in the bad place when I let a few rednecks do me out of what rightfully belongs to the Daughters. We'll fight them."

The senator looked grim. "Biggie, you don't have any idea what you're getting yourself into. This is not just a few Kemp County toughs. This organization is state-wide and growing every day. Your best bet is to call in the Department of Public Safety and back off."

Biggie had reared back in her chair and was gazing up at the stars.

"Biggie, did you hear me?"

"What? Oh, my, yes, I heard you, Lefty." She stood up and turned toward the door. "I think I'll turn in now. Do you need anything before I go?"

"Biggie, I'm serious. . . ."

But she'd already gone inside.

Before I went to my room, I stopped by Biggie's door.

"Biggie," I said, "I bet those Empire of Texas guys killed Luther. What do you bet?"

Biggie was sitting at her desk writing something.

"Could be," she said, not looking at me.

The next morning Biggie made me go with Rosebud to Les Duncan's garage to get the car fixed. I had intended on staying home and watching the talk shows on TV, but Biggie said that stuff would rot my mind. Personally, I think you can learn a lot about life from those shows, but when I tried to tell Biggie that she ignored me.

When we got to the garage, Buddy came rolling out from under Norman Thripp's 1986 Caddy. Buddy got up off the coaster he'd been lying on and wiped off his hands with a red shop rag.

"Hey, Rosebud. Hey, J.R.," he said. "I guess y'all came to get Miss Biggie's car fixed after I skint it all up."

Rosebud leaned up against the car and lit a cigar. He blew out a very big smoke ring and told Buddy that it was OK for him to fix the dent, but what we really came in for was to get the transmission flushed and a tune-up.

It's a good thing Rosebud knows so much about cars, because Biggie doesn't know a thing. She can barely drive, as anybody in Job's Crossing will tell you. Once, when we were in Houston, a cop stopped us because she was driving on that grassy strip in the middle of the avenue. Biggie explained to him that she was from the country and all those cars and trucks made her very nervous. She said she took the middle because nobody else was using it. She said it was waste like that that made our taxes go sky-high. He let her go with a warning but told her she'd have to get back down on the street like everybody else.

"Well," Biggie said, "if you can't beat um, join um."

She steered the car back to the road, gunned the engine, and commenced darting in and out between cars until we'd passed every other car on the road. All I could do was hang on tight. Frankly, I think we were lucky to get out of that town alive.

Buddy Duncan had raised the hood of Biggie's car, and he and Rosebud stood looking and poking around in the engine. I strolled around to check out the rest of the place. Mr. Duncan was sitting in his office drinking coffee with Mr. Jim Bob Matkin and Dick Little. When they saw me, Mr. Duncan got up and closed the office door — like I cared what they were talking about. I put a quarter in the gum machine and got a black gumball, which I put in my pocket to give to Biggie, who just *loves* licorice.

I spent the afternoon playing with Bingo in my room on account of I needed to conserve my energy for the big game that night. Booger lay on the bed with his ears flat.

14

Me and Rosebud and Biggie went to the game early to check out the other teams that would be playing before us. We could smell the hot dogs as soon as we came through the wire fence that goes around the ball field. DeWayne's mama, Betty Jo Davis, who is deaf and owns the beauty parlor where Biggie goes, was running the concession stand. DeWayne's sister, Angie Jo, was serving up Sno-Kones. His brother, Franklin Joe, who is not the athletic type, was taking orders and repeating them to his mama in sign language. Biggie ordered a chili dog and coffee and went up to get a seat in the stands.

"I'll have cheese fries and a Moon Pie," I said to Franklin Joe.

"No, you ain't," Rosebud said. "You won't be able to get up off the bench if you eat that. Get you a sody water and some peanuts. After the game, you can eat."

"I'll just have a rainbow Sno-Kone," I said to Angie Jo. "Put on lots of syrup."

Angie Jo scooped up a round ball of shaved ice from the cooler and laid it on top of a white paper cone. She pressed it down hard, added more ice, and took it to the spigots that held the flavored syrup.

I watched the bugs cloud around the big lights over the field while I waited, thinking about how our team didn't have a chance against the White Sox, until I heard her say, "Here you go, J.R. Lots of syrup like you wanted."

I looked at the Sno-Kone. Red, blue, and yellow syrup was dripping all around the edges of the paper cone and onto my hand.

"You sure have gotten brave since you moved to town," I said. "You used to be as spooky as a cat in a roomful of rocking chairs."

Angie Jo stuck out her tongue at me.

Angie Jo and Franklin Joe and Betty Jo, their mother, used to live in a cabin away in the woods. They never came to town, and the only human being they could ever remember seeing was Cooter McNutt, who lived nearby and is barely human himself. One day, me and Biggie happened to come across them fishing on Wooten Creek, and they were so shy, all three of them ran away. It was around that time that Biggie solved the mystery of the Wooten Creek Monster and sent Betty Jo to beauty school so they could move to town and live like regular

179

people. Now I think Angie Jo's got a crush on me.

"You said lots of syrup." Angie Jo's eyes twinkled. "OK, don't get mad. Here, I'll just put it in a Coke cup." She reached under the counter and pulled out a red-and-white Coca-Cola cup, size large, and dumped the whole mess in. "Here's a straw. Now, ain't that better?" She wiped her hands on a towel. "What can I get you, Rosebud?"

Rosebud pulled a bag of Red Man out of his pocket and winked at her. "I got all I need right here," he said.

"Girls are stupid," I said as we walked away.

"Naw," Rosebud said. "Not stupid. Just different. One of these days, you'll be mighty glad they are."

"Hey, Rosebud. Hey, J.R.," DeWayne said, coming around the corner of the bleachers eating a Dilly Bar. "Boy, are we gonna get beat tonight. Man, you should have seen them White Sox working out before this game started. Oowee! Are we gonna get slaughtered!" He took a big bite of ice cream and grinned around his chocolaty teeth.

"Humph," Rosebud said. "Get rid of that ice cream and get your gloves on. I'll toss y'all a few on the sidelines before time for our game to start."

DeWayne and I moved about twenty yards away and held our gloves up for the toss. Rosebud threw one nice and easy. I could have caught it, but DeWayne ran in front of me, tripping over my feet, and fell down. That pretty much sums up how the rest of our warm-up went. Rosebud would throw and we'd go chase the ball and throw it back to him. Finally, Rosebud gave up.

DeWayne wiped his hands on his pants. "Boy, are we gonna get beat," he said. "Are we ever bad!"

"Maybe not," I said. I'd been watching a kid I'd never seen before warming up on the pitchers' mound. The kid was wearing a Yankee uniform, and boy, did he have an arm on him. Russell Beamis, who is fourteen and big for his age, was catching, and I could see him wince every time he caught the ball. Once, he even dodged and fell over sideways when the ball came shooting toward him.

I shaded my eyes and stared at the pitcher.

"Who's tha—" I turned to Rosebud, but he was talking to one of the fathers and didn't hear me.

The White Sox were the first up to bat. As I headed out toward right field, I tried to get a look at our new pitcher, but he kept his cap pulled low over his eyes. There was something about the way he moved that was familiar, but I just couldn't put my finger on what it was. I figured he'd have to show himself when we went to bat, but instead of heading for the dugout like the rest of the team, he disappeared. I figured he'd have to come out when it was his turn to bat, but since we can't hit, the White Sox always made their three outs before his turn came up. The game was looking like a disaster. We went on with no score until the very last inning. Our only hope was that the White Sox couldn't come close to hitting off our new pitcher. He walked a couple of guys, but they never made it past second. Naturally, we didn't score. Finally, at the bottom of the ninth, I got lucky and slammed one into right field. I ran all the way to third while the team scrambled with the ball; then on the next batter up I slid home and the game was over.

Well, naturally, since I'd made the winning run, the team all crowded around, slapping me on the back and congratulating me.

"Where's the pitcher?" I asked.

"Here I am," said a voice I knew only too well, and the kid, who had been standing behind Russell Beamis, walked up to me, grinning from ear to ear.

"You!" I said. "You're the mystery pitcher?"

"You betcha," said Monica, giggling like an ape. "I fooled all of you. Come on; let's go find Rosebud and Miss Biggie. I'll bet Willie Mae's got something good to eat at your house. I'm starved. Did Miss Biggie tell you I'm spending the night with you?"

We found Rosebud talking to Mr. Dick Little, who stomped away muttering to himself just as we walked up. Biggie was already in the car when we got there.

Driving home from the game with Biggie and Rosebud up front and me and Monica in the back, Rosebud explained. He said he had gotten the idea that day at the farm when Monica was showing off by chunking peach culls at that crow.

"I seen right away that girl was a natural," he said. He grinned and the light sparkled on his gold front teeth.

"Where did you go when we got up to bat?" I asked Monica. "I never could find you when you weren't pitching."

Monica cackled. "I hid out in the girls' rest room," she said. "You didn't look there, did you?"

"Of course not. Rosebud, won't we get in trouble having a girl on our team? I bet we'll be disqualified."

"Not a chance," Biggie said. "It's already been decided in a court of law. Girls can play Little League exactly the same as boys."

"Yessiree," Rosebud said. "I done my homework. I checked up on all that. My momma didn't raise no fool. I reckoned Dick Little would have a walleyed fit, and he did. But he can squawk 'til the cows come home; we got the law on our side."

"Well, then, why didn't you tell me she was going to play, Rosebud?" I was getting mad that they'd all known and not me.

"I know," Monica said. "Psychology. Right, Rosebud? I was your secret weapon."

"You got it, young'un."

"Huh?" I said.

"Yeah," Monica said, ignoring me, "if they'd known I was just a girl, they might have thought they had a chance against me. Now we can tell. Huh, Rosebud?"

"I already did," Rosebud said. "I laid it on um right after J.R. made the winning run." His shoulders shook as he laughed without making a sound. "Ooowee, was that little Dick Little hot. He was hopping around like a Mexican jumping bean, squawkin' and cussin', threatening to call in the rules committee — or the governor, even. Then I whipped out my papers, which I had in my pocket, all ready to show him. That's when Lawyer Beamis walked up and told him he didn't have a leg to stand on."

"He said he'd call the governor?"

"That's what he said."

"Hmm," I said. "That's funny. He's getting his boys ready to join that Empire of Texas bunch, and they don't believe in the governor."

"How do you know that?" Biggie asked.

"Mr. Henderson told me," I said.

When we got home, Gilbert was sitting on the front steps waiting for us. He ran up to the car before any of us could get out.

"El senator esta perdido!" he shouted. *"Estoy muy preocupado!"* ("The senator is lost! I'm very worried.")

Rosebud opened the car door and spoke to Gilbert in his own language. I tried to understand, but Gilbert's Spanish doesn't sound a bit like Mrs. Winkle, my seventh-grade Spanish teacher. Finally, Rosebud motioned for Gilbert, who was still wagging his chin, to follow us into the house. Willie Mae had cold milk and a plate full of sand tarts waiting for us, so we all plopped down around the table and dug in. All except Gilbert. He kept pacing up and down the kitchen and jabbering in Spanish.

"Rosebud," Biggie said, "what in the name of Sam Rayburn is Gilbert talking about?"

185

Rosebud reached across me and got himself three sand tarts off the plate. "He says the senator's done disappeared. Gilbert's worried on account of he ain't in the habit of running off like that."

Biggie reached behind her and took a handful of paper napkins off the holder on the counter. She passed one to each of us. "Wipe your face. You've got a milk mustache," she said to me. Then, to Rosebud, "When did Gilbert last see Lefty?"

Rosebud spoke to Gilbert in Spanish, and Gilbert said something back to him.

"He says the senator decided to take a stroll downtown after everybody went to bed. Claimed it ud make him sleep better. He never came back."

"My daddy does that sometimes," Monica said. "One night we had to go out looking for him. We found him sleeping like a baby on top of a bale of hay. He'd been nipping on a jug of homemade whiskey Uncle Bertram gave to him. Mama like to killed him when she got him in the house."

"What'd she do?" I asked.

"Hit him upside the head with an iron skillet. . . ."

Biggie took a bite of cookie. "Lefty never came home at all?" she asked.

"Look who's talking with their mouth full," I said.

"You young'uns park your tongues," Rosebud said, then turned to Biggie. "Gilbert says his bed wasn't slept in."

Just then, Gilbert let out a long stream of Spanish. Rosebud listened and nodded his head; then Gilbert got up from the table and left by the back door. Pretty soon, we heard the senator's car start up and drive away.

"Gilbert's gone looking for him," Rosebud said.

Willie Mae got up and took another pan of cookies out of the oven. She sprinkled powdered sugar on them, then reloaded the plate. She set the plate in front of me.

"What do you think, Willie Mae?" Biggie asked. "Any ideas?"

Willie Mae nodded, looking wise as a treeful of owls. "I got ideas."

"Well?"

"You'd best go check that Dossie Phelps's place — if it ain't too late."

Willie Mae is a voodoo woman. Sometimes she knows things before they even happen.

"Uh-oh," I said.

Biggie looked sharply at Willie Mae, then shrugged her shoulders. "Well," she said, getting up from her chair, "Lefty's a grown man. I expect he can take care of himself. You kids go on up to bed. Rosebud's taking the two of you out to the farm tomorrow. J.R., you've been invited to spend the day with the Sontags."

"Yea!" I said, forgetting all about the senator.

Me and Monica went upstairs. We sat on my bed and played with Bingo for a while; then she went into the guest room to sleep.

That night, I dreamed the Empire of Texas had taken over the state. They had made all the Mexicans in Texas go back to Mexico. All the houses and other buildings were hidden by about twenty feet of grass on account of there was nobody left to do the mowing.

15

The next morning Rosebud woke us real early to come down to breakfast. He said he and Biggie had a full day and he wanted to get us out to the farm early. We were surprised to see Gilbert standing at the stove cooking breakfast. Rosebud said Willie Mae had a headache and was sleeping late. Gilbert made *migas.* If you don't know what that is, it's eggs scrambled up with peppers and onions, salsa, and pieces of corn tortilla with melted cheese on top. We had warm homemade flour tortillas to go with it. For dessert he'd fried up pieces of the tortillas until they were crispy, then sprinkled lots of sugar and cinnamon on top.

Monica poked at the eggs with her fork. "What's wrong with these eggs?"

"Just taste it, young'un," Rosebud said.

"Umm-boy!" I said. "This is good."

"Muy bueno," Monica said.

Gilbert answered with a whole stream of Mexican, and Monica answered back. I like to dropped my fork.

"How come you speak Spanish?" I asked.

189

"Because last summer Mr. Ben Birdsong had a bunch of Mexican guys helping him get in a crop of hay. He owns the pasture next to the farm," she said. "I would go over and help them most every day. I bet I could go down to Mexico and they'd never even know I wasn't a full-blooded Mexican," she bragged.

Biggie had finished her breakfast and was reading the paper as she drank the last of her coffee. "Well, looky here," she said. "You-all got your names in the paper."

"Hot-damn," Monica said. "Read it to us, Miss Biggie."

Biggie looked at Monica over her glasses, then commenced, "It says here: 'Mystery Player at Little League Tournament. Rosebud Robichaux's Yankees shut out Dick Little's White Sox in the second game of the Tri-County Little League Tournament last night. The fans were enthralled as the Yankees' new pitcher, whose identity was a mystery to all, took the mound and struck out each and every Sox. The final score was 1-0. Young J. R. Weatherford made the game's only score in the bottom of the ninth. At the end of the game, Coach Robichaux revealed that the talented pitcher was none other than young Monica Sontag of the Skunk Ridge Community in eastern Kemp County. Although it was an exciting game, it is this reporter's opinion that it is unnatural and unhealthy for a young girl to be playing ball with the boys. What are your comments? Write in and let us know.' " Biggie folded the paper and put it beside her plate. "If H.C. had any brains, he'd take them out and play with them. Did Gilbert find Lefty?"

"Nope," Rosebud said.

"How strange," Biggie said. "Ask him if Lefty's ever done this before — disappear, I mean."

Rosebud let go with a stream of Spanish, and Gilbert shook his head no.

"Well, he's a grown man," she said. "J.R., I've got a whole day of meetings and shopping ahead of me. I want you kids to get ready to go. I'll need Rosebud to drive me around as soon as he gets back from the farm."

I think country people are the luckiest people in the world. They can walk out their back door any time they feel like it and go down to the creek to fish or into the woods to shoot a deer or a squirrel for supper. Biggie says it's not all it's cracked up to be. She says there's lots of work to farming. I don't know. I've never seen Mr. Sontag do much of anything but sit around and chew

191

tobacco. The Sontags have a big barn out back, and in that barn are about fifteen cats with six toes. Biggie says that's because of inbreeding. She says there are some very famous cats in Florida just like Monica's. Biggie would have told me more about those cats, but I think she could tell I wasn't very interested. Anyway, Monica also has two goats, four milk cows and one bull, her dog, Buster, who I have already told you about, some chickens, and a mule named Lightning. One of the farm animals is mine. It is a turkey named Firman who I got for Christmas last year. He lives with Monica on account of we couldn't keep him in town. He gobbled so loud when he wanted to be fed that all the neighbors on our street complained. I guess the Sontags don't worry about the noise what with all the clucking and crowing and mooing that goes on around there. Mrs. Sontag promised me they would keep Firman until he died of old age and never even think about eating him for Thanksgiving dinner.

"What do you want to do?" Monica asked as we sat on her front steps watching Buster chase his tail. Monica thinks that dog is smart, but I'm not too sure.

"Ask your daddy if you can drive the truck out to the pasture. We can cut doughnuts."

"Can't. He's planted hay in that pasture. Besides, Daddy's gone to town in the tractor."

"Then let's take the rifle and go squirrel hunting."

"Can't do that, either. Last time I used the gun, I shot out one of the headlights in the truck."

I picked up a pecan and chunked it at Buster, who caught it in his mouth.

"Ain't he smart?" Monica said.

"I guess. How about if we try to ride those goats?"

"They won't let you. I tried. Hey, I've got it. How about if we get Mama to pack us a picnic lunch and we go down on the creek? We might even catch some fish and fry um up. Want to?"

"Sure," I said. "How are we going to get all our stuff down there if we can't take the truck?"

"Just a minute." Monica went into the house, and I heard her asking Mrs. Sontag to pack us a lunch. Then Monica came back out. "I know what we'll do. We'll take old Lightning. That mule is strong. He can take both of us — and all our stuff. Come on, let's go get the fishing gear."

In an hour, I was hanging on behind Monica as we bumped along on the back of

Lightning. A bedroll was tied on behind with all our supplies inside.

I was watching a buzzard circle overhead when Monica gave Lightning a hard kick and he commenced running across the plowed field as fast as a mule can go. I wanted to holler to make him stop, but I was too busy hanging on to say a word.

"Duck!" she yelled as we turned into the woods that run along the creek bank.

I ducked, but not soon enough; a low branch swept right past Monica and knocked me clean off. Monica pulled Lightning to a stop and looked down at me, laughing her fool head off.

"Very funny," I said, rubbing my butt. "What if I'da fell on my head?"

"But you didn't." She grinned, reaching a hand down to me. "Now get on back up. We're pretty near there. I've got a surprise for you."

We followed an old logging road down through the trees until we came to the steep banks of the creek. A big old willow was growing out over the water, and somebody had tied a rope to a fat limb. Monica jumped off Lightning and tied him in the shade of a pine tree. She took our minnow bucket down to the creek, filled it, and brought it back to the mule.

"Come on!" she yelled. And before I knew it, she had stripped off all her clothes except her underpants and was climbing the willow tree. She grabbed hold of the rope, swung out over the water, then let go and fell in with a splash.

I was already peeling off my clothes before she hit the water.

We must have been swimming for a couple of hours when Monica said, "I'm hungry. Let's see what Mama packed for us."

She climbed up on the bank and dug two towels out of the bedroll, tossing one to me. I took mine behind a tree to dry off and get dressed, even though I knew she was laughing at me for being modest. The way I figured it, swimming in your underpants is no different from wearing a bathing suit, but you don't have to go getting dressed in front of a girl.

The sun was in the middle of the sky when we opened the bedroll and unpacked our lunch. We had big slabs of ham Mr. Sontag had cured himself between slices of bread Monica's mom had just taken out of the oven that very morning. We had cupcakes, pickled okra, and a fruit jar full of sweetened iced tea. Chocolate three-layer cake for dessert. After we finished our meal, Monica pulled out a cigar and lit it with a kitchen match, then lay back on the blanket and looked up at the sky.

"Golly!" I said.

"What?" she said, blowing out a cloud of smoke.

"I didn't know you smoked cigars."

"Sure I do. Whenever I can steal one from Papa. Want a drag?"

"You bet!" I reached out my hand to take the cigar.

"Hey, look at that cloud up there. Don't it look just like Willie Mae?"

That cloud looked just exactly like Willie Mae — and she was scowling down at me, and as a cool breeze rustled the leaves overhead I could have sworn I heard a voice saying, *It ain't nice for little boys to smoke cigars.* I jerked my hand back. "I don't guess I want to after all."

"Suit yourself."

I knew Monica thought I was chicken, but she doesn't have to live with Willie Mae.

We lay still for a minute, watching the clouds, Monica puffing away on her cigar.

"Boy," I said. "You've sure got it made out here in the country. There's always something to do."

"I guess," she said. "What have you been doing all summer?"

I told her about finding Luther dead in his car and going to Hoss Henderson's house to get his bulldozer to pull the car out and about helping Paul and Silas investigate the crime scene and finding the buckle and the bloody rock. I told her about Buddy Duncan having a motorcycle wreck in front of our house and about how I'd seen him in the alley later and followed him to the Empire of Texas hideout. Then I told about how old Jim Bob Matkin caught me spying and how scared I was.

"Is that all?" she asked.

"Well, the senator came to visit. He kept flirting with Biggie all the time, which is a pretty disgusting thing for old people to be doing."

"Yuk," Monica said.

"But it gets worse," I said and told her about how me and Rosebud had caught him kissing Miss Dossie.

"Her? She don't even look clean. Did you tell Miss Biggie?"

"Yeah, I told her last night after you were asleep. She said she didn't care, that the senator always had been a ladies' man. I asked her what she thought about him disappearing. She don't seem too interested in that, either. Seems like she can't think of anything but that piece of land the Daughters are fixing up for a park." I looked across the creek. "Hey! It must be just over thataway somewhere." I pointed to a stand of pines on the opposite bank. "Remember that land the Birdsongs used to dump their eggs on?"

"Uh-huh." Monica got up and put her cigar out on a flat rock. "You want to fish some?"

"Naw," I said. My eyelids were getting heavy.

Monica came back and lay down beside me, and before long we were both sawing logs. I don't know how long we'd been that way when something woke me up. I opened my eyes and saw the sun was going down behind the stand of pines on the other side of the creek. I turned on my stomach and tried to go back to sleep. Then I heard a sound, the sound of a gun, and it wasn't any deer rifle. It was a series of rapid shots, like a machine gun.

I nudged Monica. "Wake up. Somebody's shooting!"

She opened one eye. "Hunters," she said. "They're all over these woods."

"No! Listen!"

It came again. *Bam — bam — bam.*

"Look!" She was pointing across the creek. Four figures were running, crouched

198

down along the creek bank.

We sneaked closer and hid behind a bush to watch. The men stopped running and stood in a group talking to one another.

"What do you reckon —"

"Shhh," Monica whispered. "Be quiet. Sounds carry over water."

Sure enough, pretty soon we could hear what they were saying. I recognized the voice of Jim Bob Matkin.

"Say," Monica whispered. "Ain't that that coach? Dick Little?"

I nodded. Suddenly the men all saluted one another and headed into the woods. We heard the sounds of trucks starting up.

"They're leaving," Monica said. "Bacon Road is just over that rise. They must be parked there. What do you think they're doing?"

"I know what they're doing. They're those Empire of Texas guys. They're practicing so they can take over the state. Jim Bob Matkin is going to be emperor."

"Come on!" Monica was already scrambling down the bank. "I know a place where we can cross to the other side."

I followed her down the edge of the creek until we came to a low spot where we could wade across. The water was clear and barely covered our feet; the bottom was sandy.

When we got to the other side, a path led into the piney woods. We followed the path until it stopped at a bob-wire fence. Monica crawled under and I followed.

"This is the old Birdsong land," she said.

"Ow!" I yelled. I wished I'd brought my shoes with me; the grass was full of sticker-burrs.

Monica showed me how to scrape my feet along the ground as I walked so it would sweep the stickers away. We must have looked silly, sliding across the grass like skaters, but it worked. Pretty soon we came to a clearing in the pines. After that, the walking was easier on account of the ground was covered with soft pine needles. It wasn't long before we came to a big ditch. Some-body must have been dumping trash there for a long time, because that ditch was just about full of stuff.

"See that fence over there?" Monica pointed to a broken-down fence. "On the other side, that's the old Threadgill place."

"Oh, yeah. And this must be where they used to dump all those rotten eggs. Hey, look; somebody's thrown a dead cat in there — and there's a bicycle. I bet I could fix that up and sell it."

"How you gonna get it back to the house?"

"We can tie it on the back of Lightning. It ain't very heavy." I was already starting down the side of the ditch. Just then, there was a noise down in the middle of that trash, and three possums came scuddling out. One stepped on my foot. I like to of jumped out of my skin. Naturally, Monica thought it was the funniest thing she ever saw.

"I believe that bike's too broke to fix," I said, climbing back up. "Let's go on."

We went farther into the woods. I stopped and grabbed Monica's arm. "Listen. I hear a radio!"

"Come on," Monica said. "And be quiet!"

She led the way, and as we went deeper into the woods the sound of the radio was getting louder and louder. Suddenly Monica paused and motioned me to come closer. I peered around her shoulder into a clearing in the woods. I saw four army tents, the kind with wood around the sides, and in one I could see a light, and I could hear the radio coming from it. It was playing a Garth Brooks song. In the middle of the clearing was a long table with benches along both sides. It was covered with beer cans and empty hamburger cartons.

"Duck!" Monica hissed.

Just as we ducked down behind a buckeye bush, Dick Little came out of the tent. He

201

walked over to a camp stove and lit the propane gas, threw a handful of wienies on the grill, and opened the flap to another of the tents.

It was filled to the brim with bags of fertilizer and barrels of what I figured must be some kind of chemicals.

I gripped Monica's arm. "Do you know what that is?"

"Sure, my daddy uses it on the crops, the fertilizer, that is. Not that much, though. That must be enough fertilizer to feed half the crops in Kemp County. What do you think that stuff in them barrels is?"

"I bet it's to make bombs!" I said. "They're going to blow us all to kingdom come! Let's get out of here. I've got to tell Biggie."

16

That night while we were eating supper, I told Biggie what we'd found.

"It was on *the Daughters'* property?" she said.

"Uh-huh."

Biggie stopped cutting her pork chop and looked at Rosebud.

"Miss Biggie," Rosebud said, "I think its about time you called that Ranger Upchurch. This thing's too big even for you to handle."

"You're right," she said. "I'll do that first thing tomorrow — no, I'll do it right this minute. I know I've got his home phone number around here someplace." She got up from the table and went to the little desk that she keeps right next to the back stairs. "Let's see; he lives over in Center Point, I think. Ah, here it is."

She dialed on the kitchen phone and stood talking for a few minutes and came back to the table. "He's driving over first thing tomorrow. I'm to meet him at the courthouse at nine."

I put down the pork chop bone I'd been

munching. "Biggie," I said, "did Gilbert find the senator?"

"No, and I'm beginning to worry. Fiddle! I should have done something about that today. I just don't know what happens to the time. Well, we'll stop by Dossie's tomorrow and quiz her real good. It's not like Lefty to be rude — crooked as a dog's hind leg at times, but his manners were always impeccable."

We were just finishing our peach cobbler topped with homemade ice cream when the doorbell rang.

"I'll get it!" I yelled.

When I got to the door, I found Mrs. Muckleroy there. Butch was standing behind her, and Miss Mattie and Miss Julia Lockhart were coming up the walk.

"Biggieee!" I called.

Biggie came running to the door, then glared at me when she saw who it was. "Lord, child, I almost had a heart attack. Don't scare me like that. Y'all come on in."

"What?" I said.

"Never mind. Just go help Willie Mae with the dishes. After you're through, ask Willie Mae to brew a pot of tea."

"Oh, rats," said Butch as he followed the ladies. "I was hoping we'd get some of Willie Mae's dewberry wine."

"Not today," Biggie said. "We've got serious business to discuss."

After the dishes were finished, I came back carrying the tray. They all oohed and aahed like they thought tea was the best drink in the whole world. Personally, I'd rather have root beer any old day.

"So, where have you been hiding the senator?" Mrs. Muckleroy said, glancing all around.

"We just couldn't wait another day to meet him," Miss Julia said. "I want to interview him for the paper."

All of a sudden, I noticed that these ladies were dressed up quite a bit more than they generally do on a weekday. Butch, too. He was wearing his black satin jeans with a white puffy shirt.

"It's not very nice for you to keep him all to yourself, Biggie," Miss Mattie said. "Just this very morning, Norman was saying how he'd voted for the man three times and he has not set one foot in our tearoom since he came to town." She took a sip of her wine, then blotted her lips with her napkin.

"I don't know where he is," Biggie said. "But that's not important. What is important is that we've got squatters on our property. J.R., tell these folks what you saw today."

"I saw a real neat rope swing over the creek

and Willie Mae's face in the clouds and — oh, yeah, my turkey, Firman. He's grown a lot." I covered my face to hide a grin.

"J.R.!"

"Oh. Well, those Empire of Texas guys are planning to blow up the whole town — and they've got their supplies stored on y'all's land out on the creek. Is that what you mean, Biggie?"

"Of course it is. Nobody likes a smarty-pants."

"Well, for the love of . . . What are we going to do?" Mrs. Muckleroy asked.

"Oooh," Butch said, crossing his feet at the ankles and putting his finger to his lips. "That's right scary. Do you reckon they're going to blow up our courthouse? I'd sure hate to see that. That building's got historical significance, doncha know."

"Not only that, but all the Daughters' files are stored down in the vault," Mrs. Muckleroy said.

"They might do anything," Biggie said. "That's why I've already called Ranger Upchurch. Everybody knows one Texas Ranger can take down a whole battalion of ignorant rednecks playing army in the woods."

Butch smiled. "Well, that's a relief. Now, let's all have another cup of tea."

"Indeed," Miss Julia said. "I'll just have to

wait to interview the senator, seeing as he's disappeared and all."

"I can't stay long," Miss Mattie said. "Norman's at the tearoom all by himself. Oh, well." She held out her cup for a refill. "A little work won't kill him."

Mrs. Muckleroy put her palm over her cup. "None for me," she said. "If you ask me, Willie Mae made it a little too strong."

"Suit yourself," Biggie said. "Cheers, everybody."

After the company left, I found Rosebud lounging on the front steps smoking a cigar, and it reminded me of something. I sat down beside him on the steps.

"Rosebud," I said, "do you think Willie Mae's got magical powers on account of being a voodoo woman?"

Rosebud blew a smoke ring the size of my head. "Son," he said, "I know she does. Ain't I seen it often enough? Wasn't I there the time she rescued a little boy from a wicked old witch?"

"Rosebud, there's no such thing as witches."

"Well, you just keep right on thinking that, if it makes you feel better." He took another puff off his cigar and gazed up at the moon.

"Well, what happened?"

"Go in the kitchen and pour me a cup of coffee, and I'll tell you about it."

When I came back he sipped his coffee and smacked his lips. "It went like thisaway," he said. "You see, this here kid wasn't no better than he oughta been, if you take my meaning. What I mean to say is he was always in trouble, disobeying his momma, not getting his homework in on time, staying out after dark — nothing serious, just the kind of badness that makes parents wonder how come they ever got it into their heads to have kids in the first place."

"So what happened?"

"Wellsir, one day, this kid, Gabriel Comeaux was his name, they were from Opelousas Comeauxs as I recall, he was coming home from the creek with a sack of crawdads over his shoulder when he happened to meet up with a old woman. She was hobblin' along all stooped over and leanin' on a walkin' stick and smokin' a cigar. Well, this old woman come up to Gabriel in the road and she said, 'Evenin',' and Gabriel, he said, 'Evenin',' and she said, 'Law me, I'm tired. You looks like a stout young boy. How 'bout if you he'p me over to that big rock 'side the road and I set a spell?'

"Well, like I say, Gabriel wasn't a bad boy, just mischievous, so he helped the old

208

woman set down on the rock, then picked up his sack to be on his way. That's when she said, 'Whatcha got in the sack, *cherie?*'

" 'Crawdads,' he said.

" 'Lemme look at um.'

"So Gabriel, he opened up the sack and let her take a peek. Them crawdads were just crawlin' and squirmin', each one tryin' to get on top of each other. Like some folks I know. And big? They must have been long as my hand." Rosebud held his hand in front of his face.

" 'Oowee,' she said, 'them are the finest-looking crawdads as I've seen in quite a spell. Looks like I ain't never gonna have me another crawfish pie. I done got too old to catch any. What'll you take for the sack?'

"Gabriel thought a minute. 'Mus' be five pounds in here. I'll take a dollar fifty.'

"The old woman looked sad. 'My, oh, me,' she said.

" 'I could let you have um for a dollar and a quarter,' he said.

"A big old tear rolled out of her eye.

" 'Well, I got to get a dollar for um. It taken me the best part of the day to catch um,' he said.

"She reached down in her pockets and turned them inside out, then shook her head, just as sad as she could be. 'All I got's this here magic ceegar,' she said. 'I'd sure hate to let it go, but my mouth's just a'waterin' for them crawdads.'

"Gabriel looked at the cigar. It wasn't any shorter than when he'd first met up with the old woman. 'What does it do?' he asked.

" 'You takes you a puff and closes your eyes and then makes you a wish,' she said. 'Anything you wants to wish for, it'll come true.'

"Well, old Gabriel, he grabbed that cigar and shoved the sack toward the old woman. She went off one way and Gabriel the other, just as proud as punch of his magic ceegar. Soon as the old woman was out of sight, he sat himself down on a log and put that cigar to his mouth. 'I wish I had a bicycle, a catcher's mitt, and a *ten*-pound sack of crawdads,' he said, thinking how that dumb old lady could have asked for the same thing. Then, just as he was about to take his first puff, a big black crow, the biggest he'd ever seen, came swooping down out of a live oak tree and plucked that cigar right out of his mouth. As it flew away, Gabriel heard it say, *'It ain't nice for little boys to smoke cigars.'* "

I looked hard at Rosebud, but he just flipped his cigar into the yard and stood up to go inside.

"Wait, Rosebud," I said. "You said she was a witch!"

"She was," Rosebud said, heading for the door. "She just wasn't a very good witch. If she'd been any good, she would have turned Gabriel into a possum and grabbed his sack of crawdads for herself. I reckon old Gabriel was just lucky that day — just like you." He rumpled my hair and turned toward the door.

"But you said Willie Mae saved him from a witch's spell. Seems to me like that old crow just stole away his chance to get his wishes granted."

"Well, it's plain as the nose on your face. There ain't no such thing as a magic cigar. You oughta know that. If Gabriel had taken a puff off that cigar, it might of made him sicker than a dog, and stunted his growth, too."

"So, why did Willie Mae turn herself into a crow and take it away from him?"

"Huh? Willie Mae turn herself into a crow? Did I tell you Willie Mae turned herself into a crow? You better not let her hear you say that, or she'll turn you over her knee and give you a good hiding."

I was getting mad. "Then how did she save him from a witch's spell?"

"You'll have to ask her that. I wasn't there."

With that, he disappeared into the house, slamming the door behind him.

It's not easy being a kid in this family.

17

I didn't want to go to the courthouse with Biggie, but she made me on account of I was the one that saw all the stuff those Empire of Texas guys had stored on the Daughters' land.

"It's a beautiful day," she said. "Let's walk to town."

I noticed that Biggie was wearing her Sunday dress. "How come you're so dressed up?" I asked.

Biggie turned pink. "What? This old thing? Why, I wear this all the time. You just don't notice."

Personally, I think Biggie's sweet on Ranger Upchurch. He helped out when me and Biggie found out who murdered Monk Carter, our town's last undertaker. I don't see what she sees in Upchurch. He's got red hair with gray in it, and the back of his neck is all crisscrossed with wrinkles. His ears turn down at the tops, too. I will say this, though: he's nice, and his clothes are always neat. He has creases in his western pants and shirts, and his ranger badge is shined like a brand-new dime.

Our courthouse is the biggest building in town. It has doors on all four sides, and when you walk in it's always cool and has a smell all its own, like old papers and disinfectant and stale cigar smoke. I kind of like it. I don't know why. The Department of Public Safety office where we were supposed to meet the ranger is in the basement. When Biggie pushed open the glass-topped door to the office, Ranger Upchurch was talking to John Wayne Odle, the highway patrolman. They both stood up when we came in.

"Take your seats, boys," Biggie said.

John Wayne pulled up a chair for Biggie and one for me. "How can we help you, Miss Biggie?" he asked.

Biggie sat down with her purse on her lap and crossed her feet. "It's those Empire of Texas fellows," she said. "They've overstepped themselves."

"In what way, Miss Biggie?" the ranger asked.

"Well, as you know, they've been running around town in army uniforms playing soldier for quite a while now. They think it's a big secret, but everybody in town knows what they're up to. Until now, I haven't said anything because they weren't bothering anybody. See what I mean?"

The men nodded.

"Only now," she continued, "they're beginning to get my goat. They've gone and set up their little play camp on a piece of land that belongs to the Daughters. J.R. saw it. They have a regular army post out there."

"Yeah," I said. "They're gonna build a bomb, too. I know on account of we saw a bunch of fertilizer in one of the tents — just like them guys had in Oklahoma City."

"Those," Biggie said, *"those* guys."

"We know all about that camp," the ranger said. "We take these movements seriously even though they do look like a bunch of clowns playing army. I know what they have stored out there, and so far it's nothing but fertilizer and guns, no explosives. They go out there every week or so and camp out. They practice maneuvers and calisthenics, but mostly, they just lie around and drink beer."

"Well, they'll have to drink their beer somewhere else," Biggie said, "because we're building a retreat center on that land." She leaned forward and looked the men square in the eye. "Now, what do we have to do to get them off?"

The ranger smiled. "You've sure got grit, Miss Biggie. Truth is, you don't have to do a damn thing to get them off but wait 'til they've all gone home, then go out there with a bulldozer and rake all their stuff away. They're the trespassers."

Biggie stood up. "That's all I wanted to hear." She started for the door. "Come, J.R."

The ranger followed us. "Miss Biggie," he said, "I was just informing you of your legal rights. That doesn't mean getting them off won't be a problem. Why don't you notify me or John Wayne when you get ready to do it, and we'll have some men out there to protect your 'dozer driver."

Biggie stuck her hand out. "Thanks, Red," she said. "Why don't you come over for dinner sometime? You're getting mighty lean. You need some of Willie Mae's good cooking to fatten you up a bit."

The ranger looked at Biggie. "Why, Miss Biggie, looking at your trim figure, I don't see how that's going to work. Still, I'd be grateful for a good home-cooked meal."

"Good," Biggie said. "I'll call you soon."

When we left the courthouse, the wind ruffled Biggie's hair. She looked pretty for an old woman. She started off down the sidewalk so fast I had to trot to keep up.

"Step lively," she said. "I want to see Dossie about Lefty; then we'll stop by the tearoom for lunch. While we're there, I want to fill Mattie in on what I heard from Red Upchurch. She'll be sure to spread the word to the other Daughters."

When we got to the antique shop, Miss Dossie was sweeping the glassware with a big feather duster. The dust in the air burned my nose. She looked embarrassed when she saw Biggie and started in talking real fast.

"Well, hidy, you two. Haven't seen you in quite a spell. Didn't break that brand-new platter already, did you? You sure look nice, Miss Biggie. That a new dress? What can I do for y'all?"

"First, you can put that thing down," Biggie said. "Dossie, you need to give this place a good cleaning. That bunch of turkey feathers isn't doing any good."

Miss Dossie put the duster behind the counter, and Biggie continued. "Lefty's disappeared. He's been missing for two days." She looked sharply at Miss Dossie. "Have you seen him?"

Miss Dossie turned red. "Me? Why would I see him? I don't hardly know the man."

"Dossie, we know he's been hanging around here. Now, tell us what you know. His man, Gilbert, is worried sick."

"Oh, well, he did come in here a lot at first," Dossie said, "just wanting to talk and stuff. To tell the truth, he was kind of in the way. Anyway, day before yesterday was the last time I seen him. He was standing over there by the sheet music when Mr. Hoss Henderson came in to visit the ring he's got on layaway for his wife's birthday. As I was getting it out of the safe, I saw Lefty heading down the back hall toward my health spa area. I figured he was going back there to rest until Hoss left, but while Hoss was looking at his ring some more folks came in, and I was busy for a good little while." She pushed a strand of black hair out of her eyes. "I believe that was the last time I saw Lefty, Miss Biggie."

Biggie commenced asking a bunch more questions, so I decided to go back and look at the tanning bed again. I planned to turn the thing on and see if it would tan my hands in the time it took them to get through talking. I went into the room and pushed the red button on the end, then raised the lid. After that I started screaming and screaming.

I'm not proud of it, but you would've, too, if you'd seen what I saw. When I opened up the lid of that tanning bed, I found the missing senator — and there was no mistaking the fact that he had made his final junket. He was laid out, still wearing his white suit, just like he was in his coffin, with his little bitty hands folded over his chest. Somebody had closed his eyes. I might have thought he was just sleeping except for the fact that his skin was a kind of darkish gray, like maybe whoever put him there had thought it would be a good joke to set the timer on the tanning bed for about forty-five minutes.

The women came running when they heard me scream. Biggie saw him first and covered her mouth with her hand, and Miss Dossie, who had come along behind, commenced screaming her head off.

Quick as a wink, Biggie closed the lid, took Miss Dossie by the waist, and led her back to the front of the store. She looked over her shoulder at me, and I nodded to let her know I was OK.

"Sit down on your stool, Dossie," she said, "and try to quiet down. Screaming like that's not going to bring Lefty back. Have you got any whiskey around here?"

Miss Dossie nodded and pointed toward the cash drawer. I reached in and pulled out a half-pint of Old Crow.

"Open it," Biggie instructed, and when I handed it to her she held it to Miss Dossie's lips and poured about half the bottle down her, then turned it up and took a healthy gulp for herself. She capped the bottle and turned to me. "Are you all right, honey?"

I nodded. "Biggie, do you want me to go fetch Paul and Silas?"

"No," Biggie said, sinking down on a stool next to Dossie. "First run to the courthouse and see if you can catch Ranger Upchurch before he leaves town. Then find Paul and Silas. Run as fast as you can!"

I crossed the street to the courthouse just as the ranger was getting into his car. I pointed to Miss Dossie's shop. "Biggie needs you. Hurry!" Then I ran back across the street and down the sidewalk to the police station on the corner and went in. Paul and Silas was just letting Cooter McNutt out of jail and was handing him his valuables, which consisted of a can of Skoal snuff, a pocketknife with a broken blade, and a ratty old wallet. "Come on!" I yelled. "Biggie needs you."

"In a minute, J.R.," Paul and Silas said. "Now, Cooter, you sign right here. It just says I've given you all your valuables back."

"Not so fast," Cooter said, reaching for the wallet with one grubby hand. "I got to count my money, don't I?"

"Paul and Silas," I said, grabbing his arm. "The senator's dead. He's laying in Miss Dossie's tanning bed!"

Paul and Silas got up from his desk, shoving the stuff toward Cooter, and followed me out to the street.

When we got back to the shop, the ranger was questioning Miss Dossie and making notes on a legal pad.

"Now, Miss Dossie, give me the names of everybody who came into the shop within the last two days. Can you do that?"

"I'll try," she said, "but I don't guarantee I'll remember everybody. You know, we've been running a sale this last week. Business has been right smart, doncha know." She reached for the whiskey bottle and took a slug. "Well, there was H. C. Crouch. He came in this morning to get the copy for next week's ad." She ran her hand through her hair and looked at the ranger through half-closed eyes. "That man will rob you blind."

Biggie picked up the whiskey bottle, capped it, and shoved it back in the drawer.

"Then, lemme think," Miss Dossie continued. "Oh, yeah, Miss Lonie Fulkerson, wanted to see if I had any more lace doilies. She's making a fancy quilt and sewing them on the squares. Then that new woman, Twyla Matkin, came in. She put a Limoges tea set on layaway. She was in a hurry on account of that old mean husband of hers was parked outside in the truck honking the horn. Then, oh, I don't know. I'm just so upset. Can't this wait? All I want to do is just go to the house and forget about the whole thing."

The ranger put his pad in his briefcase. "That's a good idea, Miss Dossie. You go on home. But leave me a key to the store. I'll stay until the ambulance comes. You won't be able to open up tomorrow; we'll have to seal the store off until our investigation is over."

"Whatever," she said. "Here's my extra key. Be sure and lock up when you leave." She got off her stool and stumbled a little as she left the store.

"Will she be all right?" Paul and Silas asked.

"Why don't you drive her home," Biggie said. "I'll call Brother Braudaway, her preacher, and have him go over and check on her this evening." Biggie had been wandering around the store picking up objects and laying them down while the ranger was questioning Miss Dossie. Now Biggie faced him, looking him straight in the eye. "What do you think, Red? We've had two public officials murdered here in Job's Crossing. Could it have something to do with this silly militia movement?"

222

"Possibly," the ranger said. "Biggie, I'd like to examine the body before the EMS gets here. Think you're up to coming back with me?"

Biggie looked pale but followed him toward the back. I stayed where I was. For once, I wasn't the least bit curious.

When we got home, Willie Mae was grating fresh coconut to go on top of the pies she'd left cooling on the counter. Rosebud was sitting at the table sharpening his knife.

"Where's Gilbert?" I asked. "I've got something to tell him."

"Hold your horses," Biggie said. "You're not telling him a thing." She turned to Rosebud. "Where is he?"

"He's up in the garage apartment watching the stock car races," Rosebud said. "What you got to tell him that won't wait?"

I opened my mouth to speak, but Biggie gave me a look and sank down in a chair with a big sigh. Rosebud got up and poured her a cup of coffee from the pot on the stove.

"What's wrong, Miss Biggie?"

Biggie's hand shook as she lifted her coffee cup. "Lefty's been murdered. You'd better go up and tell Gilbert." She went on to tell Rosebud how we'd found him in the tanning bed. "Somebody killed him with a blow to the back of the head."

"Just like Luther," I said. "I found him. Is there any coconut milk left?"

"What do you want me to tell Gilbert to do?" Rosebud asked. "He's gonna want to know."

"Tell him to stay put. The ranger will want to question him tomorrow. After that, he will tell Gilbert when he can leave. Then, we'll buy him a bus ticket back home, I guess. I don't know. I'm going up to my room to rest until supper."

"Can I drink the coconut milk?" I asked.

Willie Mae handed me a cup of the milk and rumpled my hair. "How you doin'?"

"Huh?"

"You OK?"

"Oh — yes'm. I'm used to finding dead bodies. I've been finding them a lot lately. Well, I guess I'll go up and see how my rats are doing."

That night I dreamed the president came to visit and I accidentally killed him with a baseball. They were going to throw me in prison for nine hundred years. I woke up screaming, and Biggie came and sat by my bed holding my hand until I went back to sleep.

18

The next morning, just as we were finishing breakfast, the doorbell rang.

"I'll get it!" I yelled, making for the front door.

It was Ranger Upchurch. He took off his cowboy hat. "Morning, J.R.," he said. "Mind if I come in?"

I stepped aside and he came into the hall.

"Biggeee!" I yelled.

Biggie forgot to say anything about my yelling when she saw the ranger, just invited him into the kitchen for coffee.

The ranger sat down at the kitchen table and stretched out his long legs in front of him. He was wearing eel skin boots. "I came by to question the senator's driver," he said. "What's his name?"

"Gilbert," I told him.

"I'll fetch him," Rosebud said and disappeared out the back door.

"But you can't talk to him," I said, "on account of he only talks Mexican."

The ranger's eyes crinkle at the corners when he smiles. "I reckon I'll get by," he said. "Seeing as how I was raised in Harlingen. That's down in the Rio Grande Valley, doncha know."

"Does everybody there speak Spanish?" I wanted to know.

"They better, if they want to get along," he said.

"J.R.," Biggie said, "most everybody is bilingual in the valley."

"I thought they were Mexican," I said.

Biggie smiled. "Never mind. I'll explain later. Here comes Rosebud with Gilbert."

The ranger took Gilbert into the dining room and shut the door. Later, when they came out and Gilbert had gone back to his garage apartment, Biggie and Ranger Upchurch took glasses of tea and went into the parlor. They didn't invite me to go with them, so I listened at the keyhole.

"Could he tell you anything?" Biggie asked.

"A good bit, actually," the ranger said. "Your senator was crooked as a bucket of fishhooks. Just about any shady political scheme you can name, he's done it. According to Gilbert, just about anybody within a hundred miles of Austin would be glad to see him in hell with his back broke."

"Well, he sure had me fooled," Biggie said. "Any particulars?"

"Plenty. Starting with Gilbert. Old Lefty found him tending bar in Matamoros back in '85 and sneaked him across the border just because he liked the way he mixed a margarita. He's been here illegally ever since. Gilbert says he'd love to go home, but the senator told him he'd have him put in jail for stealing money if he tried to leave."

"My soul," Biggie said. "Gilbert seemed so worried about him."

"He wasn't worried about his safety. He was worried because Lefty always carried all Gilbert's identification papers on his body. Gilbert couldn't even get a job without them. And he didn't have a cent of money to go home on."

"Wonder why he never told Rosebud all this?"

"He didn't know you. He figured if you were Lefty's friends, you'd probably be like him — rotten to the core."

"Poor thing," Biggie said. "What's to become of him?"

"Oh, he'll be OK. I'll retrieve his papers from the funeral home in Center Point. The problem is, I don't want to send him home to Mexico until we get this thing solved. He may have to testify in the trial. Do you suppose you could get him some kind of work here in town?"

"I'll talk to Ben Birdsong," Biggie said. "He always needs help out at the chicken plant."

"Good," the ranger said.

There was a long pause; then Biggie spoke up again. "What else did Gilbert tell you?"

"Lots," the ranger said. "But I could sure use a glass of iced tea. Think there's a chance?"

I heard Biggie get up and start toward the door, so I ran upstairs to my room before she could catch me.

After the ranger finally left, I found Biggie and Rosebud walking around the house inspecting the flower beds.

"I think we should take out these hollies and put in some pyracantha," Rosebud said, pointing toward the hedge on the side of the house. "These things done got too leggy."

Biggie cocked her head to the side. "You're right," she said. "Those need to come out. But I don't know about pyracantha. It's right outside my bedroom window. The birds will wake me up at dawn in the fall when the berries come out."

"You right about that," Rosebud said. "How about some nice variegated pittosporum? It don't make no berries."

"Good. And do you think we could put a big bed of zinnias over here in this sunny spot beside Essie Moody's fence? I just love to cut zinnias for the house."

"Sure," he said. "And how about some ornamental kale around the edges? It'll stay pretty right on into fall. Then we can take out the zinnias and put in pansies."

This kind of talk went on until I couldn't stand it one minute longer.

"Biggie," I said. "Aren't we going to help solve the murders?"

"Nope," she said. "Red's going to work on both cases, Lefty and Luther. He'll have plenty of help from Paul and Silas and the highway boys. My first priority is to get those rednecks off the Daughters' property. Red's going to be too busy to worry about that, what with these murders and all."

Rosebud bent over and plucked a cigar butt out of the flower bed. "Miss Biggie, don't you reckon you better leave that to —"

"In fact," Biggie said, ignoring him, "I've arranged a tour of the property this very afternoon. J.R., I want you to go along and show us exactly where the camp is."

"Do you need me to drive y'all, Miss Biggie?" Rosebud asked.

"No. Ruby Muckleroy's picking us up. Why don't you get started on these beds? Ask Gilbert to help. It's a cinch he could use the extra money. Go up and wash your face,

J.R. And put on your old shoes. We'll probably be walking in some mud out there."

At half past two, Mrs. Muckleroy stopped her car in front of our house and honked the horn. We had two carloads of Daughters going out to the property. Biggie sat in front with Mrs. Muckleroy while I had to sit wedged in the back between Miss Lonie and Miss Mattie. Miss Julia Lockhart and Mrs. Crews followed in another car. We drove out Birdsong Road past the Fresh as a Daisy chicken plant, then turned right on an old logging road that took us into the property.

"Now," Biggie said, getting out of the car. "J.R. can show us just where these squatters are. Be careful, girls. This grass is full of stickers. Ruby, why in the world did you wear hose?"

I scratched my head. "No, I can't show you, Biggie. Me and Monica came in from the creek side. I don't know where it is from here."

"Hmm," Biggie said, shading her eyes while she looked around the little clearing we were standing in.

"Oooh," Miss Lonie said. "Looky here. There'th dogwood tree'th all over the property. Won't thith be pretty in the thpring?"

"And all this sweet gum will be gorgeous in the fall, too," Mrs. Crews said. "And look at the smilax hanging in these trees. We always decorate our church at Christmas time with that because it stays nice and green all winter."

"And pokeberries," said Miss Mattie, pointing to a tall plant with black berries growing out of the top. "My sakes, I haven't had any pokeweed greens in I don't know how long."

"Well, you can't pick any now," Miss Julia said. "That stuff will poison you after it makes berries."

"Everybody knows that," Miss Mattie said. "My lord, Julia. I wasn't born yesterday."

"We have poke greens every spring," Mrs. Crews said. "It cleanses the system."

"How do you cook them?" Miss Lonie asked. "My mama always uthed to —"

"Come on, J.R.," Biggie said. "We'll just head for the creek, and you can lead us from there."

I followed Biggie into the woods, while the others followed. The woods got denser as we went in, and the Daughters kept stopping to talk about everything they saw growing there. Before we knew it, me and Biggie had left the other ladies a good long way behind us.

Biggie stopped on a little rise and shaded her eyes with her hand. "I think it's over that way," she said, pointing. "J.R., you climb up in that oak tree and see what you can see."

It was pretty hard, but I'm a good climber. When I got high enough, sure enough, I could see the creek about fifty yards in front of us. I scrambled down and led the way. When we got to the creek, it was easy. The camp was just to our right.

"See, Biggie?" I said. "There's their tents. Come on."

The camp was deserted, so we had a good chance to explore. There were four tents. One seemed to have been set up as their meeting place. A long table stood at one end, and pinned to the wall behind it were two maps, one of the state of Texas and the other of Kemp County. There were folding chairs in front of the table. In the rear of the tent, boxes full of canned food and flour and stuff were stacked against the wall. Pots and pans hung on a rope stretched across the canvas. The next two tents must have been where they slept on account of they were full of army cots made up real neat. In the rear tent I could see the bags of fertilizer me and Monica had spotted the other day. Beside the bags was a 100-gallon drum with MONKTON'S FUEL OIL stamped on the side and a stack of those long wooden boxes I'd seen in their hideout downtown.

Biggie was walking around the camp muttering to herself. "Would you look at this? The nerve! My soul, would you look at this?"

Suddenly something fell to the ground at my feet. I like to have jumped out of my skin, but it was only a hickory nut that a squirrel had dropped. I looked up and there he was, chattering away at me like I'd stolen his old nut. I picked up the nut and chunked it at him, then went over to the supply tent where Biggie was.

"Biggie," I said. "This is the same stuff they used to blow up that building in Oklahoma."

"Really!" Biggie said. She bent over and pulled on the lid of a wooden box that was sitting on the floor beside the oil drum. "I can't get this open. J.R., see if you can find a chisel somewhere."

I hunted around inside the tent until I came across a toolbox. I pulled out a large screwdriver. "Will this do?"

"Open it," Biggie said.

I pried open the wooden box, then jumped back. It was chock-full of dynamite sticks. I laid the lid back down real easy. "Biggie, I'm scared."

"Smart kid," said a voice behind me.

19

I sure hated to turn around, on account of I had recognized that voice. It was the voice of Jim Bob Matkin. I was shaking all over when I turned and looked into his mean gray eyes. He was wearing army fatigues with the cap pulled low over his face and shiny combat boots. He leaned toward us with clenched fists. Everything about him looked mad; only the corners of his mouth were turned up in a hateful grin.

Biggie stuck out her hand. "Good afternoon," she said in her company voice. "I don't believe we've met, Mr. Matkin, but I know your wife, Twyla." She drew herself up to her full four-foot-eleven. "She has petitioned to become a member of the James Royce Wooten Chapter of the Daughters of the Republic of Texas. I feel sure that, barring any unforeseen circumstances, she will be welcomed into our group."

Mr. Matkin didn't take her hand; he just stood there smiling that ugly smile. I noticed that a few other men dressed in army clothes had come out of the office tent and were watching from about ten feet away. I recognized Buddy Duncan and his daddy, Les, and Mr. Dick Little. Finally, Mr. Matkin turned to the others.

"What do you think, boys?" he said.

They all looked at the ground and shuffled their feet. Finally, Mr. Duncan spoke. "Miss Biggie don't mean no harm," he said. "Let um go on about their business."

Buddy nodded in agreement, but Mr. Little spoke up, saying, "As provost marshal of this camp, I say we detain these two. They have trespassed on Empire of Texas territory, and according to article II, section 32.a, of the constitution, that's a misdemeanor offense. The law says we have to hold them over for a hearing."

Biggie glared at him. "What are you saying, Dick Little?" she said. "You know good and well this is Daughters property. Why, you're the Grand Tail Twister of the Lions Club. You signed the deed, which has been legally recorded at the courthouse."

Mr. Little stepped forward. He looked Biggie in the eyes. "Legally!" he barked. "We don't recognize your deeds — or your courthouse. This here's the Empire of Texas, and before long, *we'll* be the law around here." He turned to Buddy Duncan. "Lock these prisoners in the brig."

"Huh?" Buddy said.

"The pokey! Lock um up!"

"I didn't know we had a pokey," Buddy said, looking all around the camp.

"Lock um in the supply hut," Mr. Matkin said. "It's the only place we got." He pulled a ring of keys out of his pocket and handed it to Buddy.

"We'll be going now. Come, J.R.," Biggie said, taking my arm. "And, Mr. Matkin, you'll be hearing from the Texas Rangers. We'll just see what they have to say about —"

Mr. Matkin had clapped his hand over Biggie's mouth. He picked her up, threw her over his shoulder, and marched around behind the mess tent. I followed, and Buddy Duncan followed me. Behind the mess tent was a small portable building like they sell for people to put in their backyards to store stuff in. It must have been about six by eight feet. A padlock on a chain held the door shut. Buddy opened the lock with the key, pulled open the door, and Jim Bob Matkin dumped Biggie in. I ran to Biggie and crouched down beside her as the metal door banged shut. Then we heard the chain scrape through the steel loops and the lock click in place.

"Well, I'll be switched," Biggie said, standing up and brushing herself off.

It was dark in there, but there was one

small high-up window that let in enough light for us to see a little. The floor was dirt, but covered with pine needles on account of the building had been set down under some pine trees. At first we couldn't see much, but soon our eyes got used to the dark, and we could see that the building held packages of canned foods as well as paper towels and detergent and stuff. It looked like the Empire of Texas had made a raid on Sam's Wholesale Club.

"What are we gonna do, Biggie?" I asked.

"Let me think," she said, pulling up a case of corned beef hash and plopping down on it. I found a case of peanut butter and sat facing her. She thought for a long time, then said, "Stand on a box and look out the window."

I climbed up and looked out. "All I can see is the back of a tent, Biggie."

"Can you push the window open?"

"I don't think it opens, Biggie. It looks like it's just made into the building."

"Then get down and push on the door. See what you can see from there."

I pushed on the door, and it opened about two inches, just enough for me to see a little slit of outside toward the camp. I saw Mr. Matkin, Mr. Les Duncan, Dick Little, and Buddy Duncan sitting around a picnic table in the middle of the clearing. All except Buddy had a can of beer, and they were arguing.

"I think we ought to target Camp Hatten over near Marshall," Dick Little said. "My sources tell me they got Chinamen all over the place doin' top-secret scientific experiments. Now, let me tell you fellers, when you get them Chinamen involved when we already got in bed with them Rooshkies, we're headed for world government. Sure as shit stinks!" He pounded the table with his fist, and Mr. Matkin's beer went flying in his lap.

Then it got real quiet. Everybody looked at Mr. Matkin, who slowly got up and brushed the suds out of his lap, then walked out of my sight. When he came back he was holding a fresh beer. He sat down and took a big swallow, then began to talk, real slow. "Now, get this straight, Little Dick; you ain't on a policy-making level. If I've told you once't, I've told you a hunnerd times, it ain't them others we got to worry about. Hell, they're halfway across the world. Let the U.S. government worry about the rest of the world. We ain't part of that no more. It's the goddamn *Mesicans* we got to worry about. Here in the Empire of Texas, we got to protect our borders from the Mesicans comin' over here and takin' jobs from our own white boys. Look what old Ben Birdsong's gone and done. He's got so many tamale stuffers working out there at his chicken plant, it's a wonder them birds don't all taste like chili powder."

The Little League coach had been looking down at his beer all through Mr. Matkin's speech. Finally, he said, "I wish y'all wouldn't call me Little Dick. It ain't fittin' for a full bird colonel." He pointed to a patch on his shirt in the shape of an eagle.

Mr. Crouch from the newspaper clapped him on the back. "That's OK, son. Hell, the rest of us is all generals! 'Cept for Buddy here." He pointed to the stripes on Buddy's sleeve and laughed. "Ain't that right, Sergeant?"

Buddy nodded and didn't say anything.

"Don't you worry, son," Mr. Crouch continued. "We're gonna get some more enlisted men in here for you to boss around. Fact is, we're musterin' with the unit from Cass County next week. I hear they got privates and corporals and all like that."

Mr. Matkin stood up. "Everybody up and into the operations tent," he said. "I want to go over the drill for Operation Courthouse one more time. No, not you, Buddy. You're the mess sergeant. Get busy and stir us up some supper. Wait! What's that noise?"

It was a very big machine, and it was coming our way. I could hear limbs and branches breaking in front of it, like a huge dinosaur was crashing through the woods. Then I saw it through the crack in the door. It was Mr. Hoss Henderson on his bulldozer. He'd come to clear the land like Biggie had asked him to do. Four of the men went over to talk to him, and pretty soon I heard Mr. Henderson shut off the 'dozer. They seemed to be arguing, but I couldn't hear what they were saying.

I jumped up and started banging on the wall of the little house. It was made of steel and made a good bit of noise, but Biggie grabbed my arm to stop me.

"Let go, Biggie. I gotta let Mr. Henderson know we're here."

"Shhh," Biggie said. "He can't help us. He'll only get captured, too."

I watched at the door while Mr. Henderson had a conversation with the men, then got back on his 'dozer and rode off again. As he disappeared from my view, I caught a glimpse of Mr. Matkin going after him. He was carrying a gun.

I sat back down. "There went our last chance," I said.

Biggie patted me on the arm. "Don't

worry, honey. Pretty soon Rosebud and Ranger Upchurch will come looking for us. By now, the girls will have already told them we're lost. I'm sure of it."

"Oh." I sat back down on my peanut butter jars, and Biggie put her chin in her hand and commenced thinking again.

Pretty soon, the smell of barbecue came drifting over from the clearing. It made me think about how Willie Mae was probably setting the table for supper this very minute. My stomach commenced growling real loud, but Biggie didn't seem to notice. She was still thinking.

Now it was beginning to get dark. I could hear the clanking of spoons and forks against metal plates as the men ate their supper. They were talking, but I didn't even try to hear what they were saying. I was too hungry. After a while, they scraped their scraps on the ground right outside the little house and went inside the tents.

"Biggie, I'm hungry, and I've got to go to the bathroom real bad."

"Hush," Biggie said. "Don't think about it. I think I know who did the murders."

"What? Biggie, we know who did it. These Empire of Texas guys, of course. But what good does that do? We're prisoners of war, Biggie."

20

Biggie didn't say anything, just kept sitting still with her chin in her hands like she does when she's thinking hard. I could hear the men in their tents talking for a while; then the lights went out and all I heard was the sound of an owl in the woods and, in the distance, an old bullfrog in the creek going *chug-a-rum, chug-a-rum*. I pushed together a pile of pine needles and lay down, figuring I might as well be comfortable while I waited to be killed. I was just about to drift off to sleep when I heard something outside the building. Someone opened the padlock and the door opened slowly. I could see Buddy Duncan silhouetted in the moonlight. He was holding something in his hand.

"Don't be afraid," he said. "I brought y'all some food and a soda pop." He looked back at the tents, then hurried up and shut the door. "It's just some old cold ribs, and you'll have to eat um in the dark."

Biggie took the paper sack he'd brought and took out a rib, then handed the sack to me. I opened my soda and took a big gulp, then started chewing on a piece of meat.

Biggie pulled over a box and motioned for Buddy to sit down. "Why are you here, Buddy?" she asked.

"Because you've been good to me, Miss Biggie. I just couldn't go to sleep knowing y'all were out here probably hungry and thirsty."

"And needing to go to the bathroom," I said.

"That's nice," Biggie said. "But that's not what I mean. I mean why are you here with these men? You're not like them."

Buddy turned red in the face and looked at Biggie with sad eyes. Then he squared his shoulders and tried to look tough, like the others. "Oh, yes, I am," Buddy said. "The government is bad. You know all those bombings they've been having? Mr. Matkin says the U.S. government done the Oklahoma City bombing on account of it's run by a bunch of Jews that just want to get rid of all us good Christians. He says they bombed that World Trade Center in New York City so they could lay it off on the Ay-rabs!" Buddy's voice was shaking.

Then Biggie did something I never would have expected. She scooted over close to Buddy and wrapped her arms around him. "Honey," she said, "I've known you all your life. Why, I even taught you in Sunday school. Now tell Biggie why you're sitting here talking like that crazy Jim Bob Matkin."

Buddy was quiet for a long time, just letting Biggie hold him. Then words started gushing out of him. It was like he had to get it said real fast before he lost his nerve.

"You're right, Miss Biggie," he said. "I don't believe like them. Why, I used to be an Eagle Scout. You remember? And I played in the band in junior high — first chair trumpet — and I was class favorite my freshman year in high school."

"I remember all of it," Biggie said. "Your mama was so proud."

"Yes'm. Well, it's that Mr. Matkin. He's bad, Miss Biggie. Real bad. And he's got something on my daddy that's caused me and him to have to join up with them."

"What?"

"I can't tell you."

"Yes, you can."

"No'm. You don't know those fellers."

"Buddy Duncan, you tell me this very minute!"

When Biggie uses that tone, everybody minds.

"Yes'm. I guess I can tell you, but don't go thinking you can do anything about it, because can't nobody go up against Jim Bob

Matkin. Well, here goes. It all started when my daddy was in the army — in Vietnam. He was a sergeant in charge of the motor pool at a base outside of Saigon. Bad luck for my dad, Jim Bob Matkin happened to be stationed there, too. He was in the MPs."

"Military Police."

"Yes'm. Well, my daddy's always been good with business. You know, he makes a nice living with the gas station and garage."

"Everybody respects your daddy," Biggie said. "Your mama, too."

"I know. Daddy's a deacon in the church, and Mama's been president of her Women's Circle for I don't know how long."

"So, what happened between your daddy and Matkin?"

"Well, the way my daddy tells it, there was this corporal in the motor pool. He was a good mechanic, but crooked. He took to stealing parts. Him and his buddies would sneak them on empty cargo planes going back home, and their partners stateside would sell them to civilians that didn't care where they came from as long as the price was right. Well, my daddy found out and reported it to his commanding officer. The CO went to the provost marshal, who turned the case over to —"

"I know," I said. "Jim Bob Matkin."

"Right. And Mr. Matkin turned the whole thing around and made it look like my daddy had done it on account of Mr. Matkin had decided to cut himself in on the deal. Daddy was court-martialed and they kicked him out of the army, and Mr. Matkin and that crooked mechanic went right on stealing army parts and selling them stateside. Apparently, Mr. Matkin came out of the war a rich man. My daddy's reputation was ruined because of that man. I hate him, Miss Biggie, but I've got to go along with him or everything my daddy and mama have worked for here in Job's Crossing will be gone."

"My soul," Biggie said. "That's some story. So then I guess when Matkin came to town, he just blackmailed your daddy into joining their little army?"

"Yes'm. And me, too."

"I just remembered something," Biggie said. "Something about you getting into trouble over in Longview. Hubcaps or something. Does that have anything to do with all this?"

"In a way," Buddy said. "I didn't do anything wrong. Me and some guys went to the picture show over there, and as we came out and were going to our car a feller started shouting that we had stolen his hubcaps.

Well, we said we didn't know anything about it, and he said we'd done it. You know how it is; one thing led to another, and a fight was about to break out when the Longview police showed up. Boy, were we surprised when they searched our car and found a bunch of hubcaps on the backseat floorboard. We were plumb bumfuzzled, Miss Biggie. We'd never seen those hubcaps before and didn't have a clue how they'd gotten into our car. The Longview police took us to jail, and my folks had to come bail us out. The next day, Mr. Matkin let my daddy know that that was just a warning — that he'd better go along or something worse could happen. That's when we both figured we'd better sign on."

"There's nothing so bad it can't be fixed," Biggie said. "Buddy, let us out of here, and I promise Jim Bob Matkin will never bother you again. I swear it."

Buddy jumped to his feet. "I can't, Miss Biggie. You don't know what you're asking. I gotta go right now!"

With that, he went barreling out the door.

"Well," Biggie said. "Bless Pat!"

I must have dozed off sitting on my peanut butter case. When I looked out the window, the night was nearly over. A gray glow was starting to form over the pine needles covering the dirt floor. There was something about that floor — something important that my tired mind just couldn't get a grip on. Biggie had gone back to her thinking, so I lay down on the floor hoping I might get a little more sleep before they came to kill us, but I couldn't get comfortable. I dug my fingers through the pine straw into the soft, damp ground underneath, and that's when I got the idea that saved our lives. I sat up and looked around the building. It was only about six feet square but was full of all kinds of stuff. I got up and commenced feeling my way around the walls. There must be something I could use — a tool of some kind.

"J.R., what are you doing?" Biggie asked. "How can I think with you jumping around like a flea?"

"Biggie, I got an idea — and I just found what I need." My hand had just fallen on a long handle propped in one corner. It was a shovel! "Biggie, we can dig our way out of here, but we got to hurry. It's almost day." I was already digging as fast as I could along the wall that faced away from the camp.

"My soul, you're right," Biggie said. She found a flat rock and started digging along with me.

It didn't take long before we had a hole big enough to squeeze through. Biggie went first; then I followed. I was halfway through when I heard a sound that made my heart pound. It was the crack of somebody stepping on a dry twig. I froze and shut my eyes tight. The next thing I knew, two big hands had grabbed me by the shoulders and pulled me the rest of the way out and set me down on the ground.

21

I sat still with my eyes squeezed shut waiting for whatever it was they were going to do to me. My heart was pounding so hard I could feel my body jerk with each beat. Then the hands lifted me to my feet, and I heard a familiar voice saying, "Ain't gonna do you no good to sull up like a possum, boy."

I opened my eyes and saw Biggie tearing across the clearing into the woods behind the camp and Rosebud standing over me. He took me by the hand, and we followed her. We soon overtook her and now were were leading the way. My legs moved with no effort at all. I was so happy to be free, I thought I could probably just take off and fly. But it didn't last long enough. Just as we rounded a curve around a big sycamore tree, a steely voice said, "Freeze!"

I stopped in my tracks, and Rosebud put his hand on my shoulder. We were staring into the gun of Jim Bob Matkin. Beside him stood H. C. Crouch, who was holding a trio of dead squirrels in one hand and a rifle in the other. Neither of them said another word, just motioned with their guns, and we all started back toward their camp. My legs didn't feel so light anymore. All of a sudden, I was so tired I had trouble putting one foot in front of the other. I couldn't stop the tears that were running down my face.

When we got back to camp, Mr. Matkin finally spoke. He fixed his pig eyes on Biggie and growled at her.

"So, Miz High-and-Mighty sent for her nigger to come rescue her from the bad old soldiers. Ain't that right?"

Biggie didn't answer. I sneaked a peek at Rosebud and saw fire in his eyes, but he didn't say a word, just stood on the balls of his feet like a panther about to spring. I saw his hands clench into fists and the muscles in his forearms ripple.

The others came out of their tents and made a circle around us. I looked at Buddy Duncan, but he wouldn't look back. He was carrying an assault rifle just like the others and had it aimed our way.

I couldn't stand it any longer. "What are you going to do with us?" I asked. My voice came out all quivery.

Mr. Matkin laughed, and it sounded like a file against steel. "Haw! Outta the mouths of babes. What are we gonna do with you? I'll tell you, son. We're gonna execute you —

that's what we're gonna do. We're gonna stand the whole bunch of you up against an old-timey firing squad."

"You'll never get away with it," Biggie said. "Right this minute, the Texas Rangers are looking for us. They know where this camp is."

"Sure, they know," he said. "Do you think I care? It's the right of every citizen to keep and bear arms. They can't touch us — and they ain't never gonna find your bodies, on account of we're gonna load your bodies in my bass boat and take you to the deepest part of the lake. We're gonna weigh you down with boat anchors so's your bodies won't never come up — or if they do, by that time, *we'll* be the law around here. Now then, Little Dick, you get over here and tie these folks up until I eat me some breakfast. Then we'll take care of business."

Mr. Little picked up a rope that was hanging on a tent pole and started toward us.

Suddenly Buddy Duncan stepped forward. He turned and aimed his gun toward the explosive tent and yelled, "Run!"

We ran for the woods, and as we ran I heard the rat-a-tat of Buddy's gun, then the loudest explosion I'd ever heard. I looked over my shoulder and saw a cloud of black smoke and fire billowing from the camp. We ran as fast as we could until we were deep into the woods. We didn't stop until we came to a clearing along the creek bank and fell to the ground panting. Then I heard another familiar voice.

"What took y'all so long?" a voice said from above us.

I looked up to see Monica sitting in the crotch of a live oak tree. "I was startin' to worry. I heard the explosion and saw the smoke." She shinnied to the ground and stood grinning at me. "Looks like I'm all the time having to rescue you, J.R.," she said.

I didn't argue, just sat still while Rosebud told her what had happened. I was still trying to get used to the idea that we were really free this time.

Biggie stood on tiptoe and kissed Rosebud on the cheek. "Now," she said, "let's get out of here. I want a good bath and breakfast."

"It's a good little piece to the car, Miss Biggie," Rosebud said. "Don't you want to rest a minute?"

"I've been resting all night," she answered. "I want to go home."

"Me, too!" I said.

Monica led the way. The walking was easy for a while as we followed the creek bank. Then she veered into the woods again. The sky had turned gray, and I could see little streaks of pink as we turned east.

"Wait a minute," I said. "Town's the other way. We're going back toward the camp."

"Not for long," Rosebud said.

I ran past Rosebud and Biggie to catch up with Monica. Just as I got to her, she tripped on what looked like a log and fell flat on her face.

I was just opening my mouth to kid her about being clumsy on account of she'd been such a smarty-pants a while back when I saw that she hadn't fallen over a log at all. It was a body facedown across the path — a body dressed in overalls with one strap hanging loose. It was Mr. Hoss Henderson.

Rosebud knelt down beside him and felt his neck. "He's breathing," he said. "But somebody's shot a hole in his shoulder. Looks like he's lost a right smart amount of blood. Can y'all help me turn him over?"

Between the four of us, we got Mr. Henderson turned on his back, and Biggie took a handkerchief out of her pocket and had started to brush the dirt off his face when she jerked her hand back.

"Praise Jesus," she said. "He's covered in fire ants. Hurry! We've got to move him and get his clothes off."

Rosebud took Mr. Henderson's shoulders while Biggie took his legs and me and

Monica both grabbed an arm, and we drug him a good six feet away from the spot where he'd been lying. Sure enough, the ground was swarming with ants, and they were crawling off his body onto our hands.

"Quick!" Biggie said. "Get his clothes off. J.R., you and Monica get his shoes off so Rosebud can pull down his pants." She was unbuttoning Mr. Henderson's shirt as she talked.

We went to work on Mr. Henderson, only stopping to brush the ants off us when the stings got too bad. I remembered the time I'd seen a dead frog at the pond in the park. It was covered with ants, and as I watched, they swarmed over it until nothing was left but a pile of bones. Our teacher told us that fire ants came to this country in fruit shipments from South America. Now they've mated with the native ants so that all our ants in Texas are fire ants and, believe you me, they can sting!

We pulled off each piece of clothes and threw them in a pile. At last, Rosebud raised Mr. Henderson's chest and lifted his shirt off while me and Monica pulled his shorts down over his feet. I guess we were so busy, we hadn't taken the time to pay attention to his body, because when the last article of clothes was off we all looked down at once and let out a gasp of surprise.

Mr. Henderson wasn't a mister at all. Mr. Henderson was a woman.

Quick as a flash, Biggie jerked off her windbreaker and spread it over Henderson's private parts while Rosebud wriggled out of his shirt and covered the chest. Then we all stood looking down at her. Nobody could think of a thing to say.

Naturally, Monica was the first to speak up. "Hey," she said, "I bet I know what this is. I bet this is one of those hermorpha . . . you know, like that person we saw at the freak show last year at Pioneer Days. You remember, J.R.?"

I didn't answer, just walked a few feet away and stood looking off down the path. I'd never seen a naked woman before and didn't want to see another one for maybe my whole life. I kept seeing that white flesh and those old saggy bosoms lying across her chest with blood running down between them and fire ant bites all over the place. It was awful — almost worse than finding a dead body.

When I finally did go back to the others, Biggie was holding a handkerchief over the wound in the person that used to be Mr. Henderson, and Rosebud was getting ready to go back to where he'd parked the car.

"Use the car phone to call for help,"

Biggie said, "then look in the glove compartment. I think I left a can of insect repellent in there from the last time we went fishing."

"Yes'm," Rosebud said and started to sprint down the path.

"I'm going, too!" I yelled, and took off after him like a scalded cat.

It was noon before we finally got home. Biggie and I ate bowls of Willie Mae's homemade chicken soup with glasses of cold sweet milk and then went upstairs for baths and a long nap.

When I woke up, the shadows were long across my bedspread, and I could see the red setting sun outside my window. Booger was curled up behind my knees with his head resting on my leg. I reached down to scratch his ear and snuggled down deeper in my bed, thinking I'd just stay there until morning. Then I smelled something — something that made me jump out of bed and start pulling on my clothes. Willie Mae had made her famous special-occasion gumbo. I took a deep breath and pictured the oysters and bits of crabmeat and chicken and andouille sausage floating around in that yummy dark gravy. I took another deep breath and smelled fresh-baked French bread.

Biggie and Rosebud were already sitting at the kitchen table drinking red wine and eating cheese straws still warm and crisp from the pan when I came in.

I plopped down in a chair and reached for a cheese straw. Then something happened that surprised me a good deal. Willie Mae opened the refrigerator and took out an icy-cold Big Red and set it down in front of me. Willie Mae usually makes a face when I ask for Big Red. She says it ain't nothing but sugar water and chemicals and will stunt my growth. She didn't say a word, just hugged my head so tight I thought I'd smother before she went back to slicing the bread. I guess she must've been happy about me and Biggie escaping from the Empire of Texas. Willie Mae doesn't say much, but she has her ways of letting you know how she feels.

After supper, when we were all so full of gumbo we couldn't move, we sat around the table and Biggie told Willie Mae the whole story, from the time we were captured until we found out Mr. Henderson wasn't a mister.

Willie Mae listened and nodded her head, not saying a word. When Biggie finished, Willie Mae said, "Now you know who done the murders."

"Yep," Biggie said. She pulled the little

piece of metal I'd found at Luther's murder scene out of her pocket and set it on the table. "Now I know."

22

The next morning it rained. Great big pounding drops that caused rivers in the gutters and made the low spot in our side yard look like a pond. Biggie, Rosebud, and I stood on the front porch enjoying the cool breeze and the fresh smell that rain in summer brings.

"Miss Biggie, what would you think if I had Rooster Collins bring over some fill dirt to level that dip in the yard?"

"I think it won't help much," Biggie said. "Back in my grandmother's day, there used to be a cistern there."

"Miss Biggie, I reckon it could be done. You just gotta —"

"There comes the ranger," I said pointing to a tan-colored car pulling up at the curb.

Ranger Upchurch stepped out wearing a raincoat. A gray plastic hat cover protected his Stetson. When he got to the porch, he took off his coat and laid it across a wicker chair and set his hat on top of the coat. He had a little groove in his hair where the hat had been.

"Morning, Red," Biggie said. "Come in and have some coffee and a sweet roll and tell us all you know."

"That's why I'm here, Biggie," he said, holding the screen door for Biggie to go in.

Me and Rosebud followed, and we all took seats around the kitchen table. I was anxious to hear about the explosion in the army camp, but naturally, Biggie took control of the conversation.

"How is Hoss?"

The ranger had his elbows on the table and was holding his coffee cup in both hands. He took a sip, then commenced talking. "He'll be scratching like a hen after grubs for a good long time — from the ant bites, doncha know. We took him over to Center Point to the emergency room. The doc gave him some salve for the bites and bandaged up his wound. Fortunately, it just grazed his shoulder. A few inches lower and he would have got it in the lung."

"He's a she," I said.

Biggie gave me a look, then reached for a cinnamon roll. "Is he in the hospital?"

"Oh, no. Doc said there was no need for that. They sent him home in the ambulance, though. His wife pitched quite a hissy when she saw the ambulance pulling up in the yard. It took a while to get it into her head that he wasn't hurt bad."

"Poor thing," Biggie said. "I might just run out there with some of Willie Mae's chicken soup this afternoon. Care to come along?"

"Reckon I ought to," the ranger said. "You going to take along the . . ." He looked at me and Rosebud.

"Right," Biggie said. "Now tell us about the camp. Anybody hurt bad?"

The ranger got up and refilled his coffee cup from the stove, then sat back down, turning his chair sideways so he faced Biggie. "Jim Bob Matkin and H. C. Crouch are dead, Dick Little has third-degree burns over half his body, and Buddy Duncan got hit in the head with a beam. He's in ICU at the hospital. They don't know whether he'll pull through or not. Les got out with a sprained wrist and scratches. He and Mrs. Duncan are at the hospital with Buddy."

"My soul," Biggie said.

"Buddy saved our lives," I said. "Biggie, you better tell the ranger what Buddy told us about his daddy."

"I know the story," the ranger said. "Les told me all about it last night while he was waiting for arraignment."

Willie Mae had been peeling potatoes at the sink. "Y'all better get out of my kitchen if you expects any lunch around here," she said.

Naturally, we all got up and headed out the door. Willie Mae means what she says. Biggie followed the ranger to the front door, and they stood there talking real soft. I went up to my room to clean out my rat cage, and Rosebud headed for the garage.

For lunch we had fried eggplant, baby new potatoes with sour cream sauce, fresh green beans cooked with ham hock, crowder peas, sliced tomatoes and cucumbers, corn bread, and tea. I saw a peach pie cooling on the counter.

"Where's the meat?" I asked.

"Under your hair," Willie Mae said.

"Huh?"

"J.R., there's enough good food here for three boys. Now just eat your lunch and keep quiet," Biggie said.

I ate three pieces of fried eggplant, and I've got to admit it tasted a good bit like meat.

After lunch, Biggie got up and commenced putting things in the purple tote bag she got last fall at the last Daughters convention in San Antonio. "J.R.," she said, "where did you put that old Wills Point annual you got at Dossie's place?"

"I thought we were going to see the Hendersons," I said.

"We are. I want to take that with me."

"How come?"

"Because I want to show it to Hoss. Now where is it?"

I jumped up and ran to my room and came back carrying the book just as Biggie was stuffing a large jar of chicken soup into her bag. She glanced up at the teapot clock over the sink. "Two o'clock. We'd better get going." She took the book from me and shoved it into the bag.

I thought about how Hoss Henderson had looked lying there naked on the ground. "Biggie, I thought I'd just stay home and, uh, clean my room. It's a mess, Biggie."

Biggie didn't say anything, just gave me a sharp look.

"What?" I said.

"J.R., I need you to go with me."

"Yes'm."

Mrs. Henderson's eyes were all red when she greeted us at the door. She asked us to come inside but wouldn't look right directly at us, and her hand shook on the doorknob. Biggie handed her the soup, and Mrs. Henderson led us to the back room where Hoss was propped up in an iron bed that had once been painted white. Now it was peeling and little polka dots of rust showed through the paint. A homemade quilt was draped across the foot of the bed. There was an old-timey marble-topped dresser against the wall. On it were several bottles of medicine and some old family pictures. I noticed another picture of Hoss's sister beside one of Mrs. Henderson when she was a girl. They were in matching frames. Hoss had a bandage on her shoulder and looked like a ghost on account of she was covered from head to toe with calamine lotion. She was wearing a T-shirt that said: BRANSON, MISSOURI, NASHVILLE OF THE OZARKS on it and men's pajama bottoms. Her overalls had been washed and were hanging on a hook beside the door. She looked startled when we came in.

"Relax, Hoss," Biggie said, taking a seat in the chair Mrs. Henderson had pushed up next to the bed. "We brought you some of Willie Mae's good chicken soup. It'll have you up and plowing in no time."

"Miss Biggie, you didn't have to —"

Just then there was a knock on the front door, and Mrs. Henderson, who had been fussing around the room, ran to answer it. She came back leading Ranger Upchurch and Paul and Silas. She perched on the foot of the bed, looking white as a sheet. Her hands shook as she fiddled with the hem of her dress. The men stood leaning against the wall. Hoss, who had been sitting up in bed, shrank back against the pillows. I could have sworn she got smaller.

"You know?" she asked in a quivery voice.

"I know everything," Biggie said.

Mrs. Henderson looked like a startled deer. "Everything?"

Biggie nodded.

Hoss spoke up. "There ain't no law against dressing up like a man, is there?" She looked at the ranger, who shook his head.

"No," Biggie said, "there's no law against that. There's no law against holding yourselves up to the community as husband and wife, either, as long as you don't use it to defraud anybody. But there is a law against murder."

The room got real quiet. Mrs. Henderson gripped the bedpost like it was all that was holding her up. Finally, a rooster crowed outside, breaking the silence.

Paul and Silas stepped forward and stood at the foot of the bed. "You have the right to keep silent —"

"I don't need that," Hoss said. "Me and Freda, we've kept silent long enough. Now's the time to tell it."

"Hoss!" Mrs. Henderson said.

"No, sugar, it's over. We done wrong, and now we got to pay." Hoss sat up in the bed and began to talk. "I've always been plug-ugly, no doubt about that. But as a girl — well, in school the kids all called me Alice the Goon. That was a ugly old character in the funny papers. She was tall and hairy, just like me. I didn't have any friends at all. Not until Freda moved to town. She never seemed to notice how ugly I was. She's got the kindest heart in the whole world, I reckon. Even I don't know why she reached out to me. It made the others just laugh and poke fun at her, too."

"I seen what was inside," Mrs. Henderson said, "the way she could sense how you were feeling and always say the right thing. And the gentle way she treated animals and little kids."

"When we got to high school," Hoss continued, "I was already more than six feet tall. Well, one day, the girls' coach approached me about going out for the basketball team. Naturally, I could play rings around all them other girls. After I joined the team, we won District four years running."

"Then they all changed their tune," Mrs. Henderson said.

"That's right. But by that time, I didn't care about any of um. Freda had stood by me from the git-go, and she was all I cared about."

"We knew we'd go to hell for it," Mrs. Henderson said, "but we fell in love with each other. We fought it — lordy, did we!"

"After graduation, I joined the army," Hoss said. "Back then, women didn't do much except typing and filing and such work as that. They sent me to Guam, where I was secretary to a chaplain. Well, one day, I was feeling down on account of missing Freda so, and I just busted out bawling right in the middle of typing a report. Wellsir, Reverend Elkins, that was his name, he come over and put his hand on my shoulder and wanted to know what was the matter. Before I knew it, I had spilled out the whole story about me and Freda. Soon as I finished talking, I commenced to shaking on account of I figured right then and there he was gonna fire me or court-martial me or give me a bad conduct discharge." Hoss looked out the window like she wasn't in that room anymore, like she was far, far away. "You know what he said? He said God is love and love can't never be bad. I hadn't never heard anything like that before. My heart just spilled over with relief."

Mrs. Henderson took Hoss's hand in hers. "So when Hoss come back home, we made it up that he'd just play like he was a man and we'd go somewhere where nobody knew us and we could be together forever and ever. It worked just fine until Luther taken to reading everybody's mail and happened to see an invitation we got from the old high school telling about a reunion they were having last fall. Somebody had put in a picture of Hoss in his basketball uniform. Naturally, we told him it was Hoss's sister, but he wouldn't believe it. Kept asking all kinds of questions and staring at Hoss like he was trying to see under his clothes. Naturally, we knew it ud be all over town before too long."

"That's when I made it up how I'd get rid of Luther," Hoss said.

"So you hit him in the head and drove his car into the ditch," Biggie said.

"How'd you find out, Miss Biggie?" Hoss asked.

Biggie reached into her bag and pulled out the metal thing I'd found at the wreck site, then got up and walked over to the hook where Hoss's overalls hung. She held it up to the one buckle that was left, and sure enough, the piece of metal was a perfect mate for that buckle.

"I could of lost that while I was pulling the car out, couldn't I?" Mr. Henderson said.

"Uh-uh," I said. "I remember; you had to pull up your strap when you got out of your chair that day. You only had one strap."

Hoss hung her head.

Biggie didn't say anything, just reached into her bag again and pulled out my Wills Point annual. Mrs. Henderson reached for it.

"Who would of thought of it?" she said. "We lost ours years ago. Who'd have thought one of these old books would make it all the way to Job's Crossing?"

"So, you killed Lefty because he recognized you," Biggie said.

"Yes'm. I seen him in that Miss Dossie's shop. He didn't say nothing at first, just looked at me with that same nasty grin that he had when we was back in school. I think Lefty was jealous on account of him being just a little peckerwood and wanting to play sports, and here was me, a girl, bigger'n him and better at sports than him. He was the ringleader of all my misery in that school. Yes'm, I killed him."

Biggie stood up. "Murder's wrong," she said. "You killed two people when all you would have had to do was tell the truth. You underestimated the folks here in Job's Crossing." She started for the door. "Come, J.R. We'll leave these two to the law."

Ranger Upchurch and Paul and Silas followed us out to the front porch.

"What will you do with Hoss?" Biggie

asked. "She's not well enough to go to jail."

"I'll keep Paul and Silas here to watch the house from the road for a couple of days. By that time, we should be able to take her in for an arraignment."

Independence Day

Biggie and the Daughters decided to have the Fourth of July celebration at the city park. They had hoped to have it at the new Daughters' Retreat Center, but since Hoss Henderson was in jail and couldn't do the dirt work, they had to hire somebody from Center Point to do the job, and it wasn't finished in time. The park looked like a tornado had ripped through a flag factory when we drove up and parked by the curb. Flags were hanging from every tree and draped over the gazebo. Little flags were planted along all the paths and in the new flower beds that surrounded Luther's memorial tree. Some of the Daughters wanted to dress up like colonial ladies, but Biggie put a stop to that. She said they weren't DARs but Daughters of the Republic of Texas and there wasn't any Texas in 1776. Mrs. Muckleroy got all huffy and said *she* was a DAR. In fact, her mother had been a Daughter of the Magna Carta. Naturally, Biggie won and the ladies all wore their regular clothes.

Tables were set up under the trees, and

every family brought a picnic lunch. Monica and I helped Willie Mae set out our food.

"Ooo-wee," Monica said. "I'm gonna eat about six of those deviled eggs. That's my favorite thing in the whole world."

"Get your hands out of them eggs and set this ham down there on the end," Willie Mae said. She handed me a bowl of potato salad and pointed to the end of the table, where Biggie was sitting drinking tea and talking to a crowd of folks that were gathered around her.

"So," Butch was saying, "you say Mrs. Hoss got off?"

"Yep," Biggie said. "She didn't really know what was going on until after the fact. Hoss didn't want her involved. She's moved to Gainesville to be near Hoss while he . . . she . . . serves her term. With good behavior, she could be released in seven years. Of course, that would depend on the parole board."

"How's Buddy Duncan?" Miss Julia asked.

"He'll live," Biggie said. "But the boy's got months of rehabilitation ahead of him. Les pled guilty, and the judge gave him probation."

"Good," Miss Lonie said. "They never meant to hurt anybody, I'm thure. And nobody can fix carth like Les can. I juth don't know what I'd do if I had to take my car to

Center Point all the time."

Just then, Paul and Silas came walking by. He was dressed in a gray postman's uniform, and Meredith Michelle was hanging on his arm.

"Oooh," Butch said. "I just love a man in uniform."

"Well, I hope you will love yourself in one," Biggie said. "Because now that Paul and Silas has taken Luther's job, you'll have to fill in as police chief until we find a permanent one."

"Oh, Biggie, I don't think I'll have the time. You know, my florist business is just booming! And before you know it, the holidays will be coming up. I'm planning to be real busy, Biggie."

"I've talked to the city council," Biggie said, "and they've authorized a generous budget for new uniforms. But if you can't do it, I'm sure we can —"

"Let me think about it," Butch said. "You know me, Biggie. I just love doing my civic duty and all. . . ."

"Fine," Biggie said. "Listen; the band's starting to play. Everybody, on your feet. They're playing the national anthem!"

The employees of Thorndike Press hope you have enjoyed this Large Print book. All our Large Print titles are designed for easy reading, and all our books are made to last. Other Thorndike Press Large Print books are available at your library, through selected bookstores, or directly from us.

For information about titles, please call:

(800) 223-1244

To share your comments, please write:

Publisher
Thorndike Press
P.O. Box 159
Thorndike, Maine 04986